The Egypt Game

THIS BOOK BELONGS TO

Megan Welsh

The Egypt Game

ZILPHA KEATLEY SNYDER

Drawings by Alton Raible

A YEARLING BOOK

**To the boys and girls I knew at Washington School
and to Susan and Tammy for the loan of some secrets.**

Published by
Bantam Doubleday Dell Books for Young Readers
a division of
Bantam Doubleday Dell Publishing Group, Inc.
1540 Broadway
New York, New York 10036

The trademarks Yearling® and Dell® are registered in the U.S. Patent
and Trademark Office and in other countries.

ISBN: 0-440-22025-4

Reprinted by arrangement with Atheneum Publishers.

Printed in the United States of America

Two Previous Editions

June 1996

10 9 8 7 6 5 4 3 2 1

OPM

Contents

The Egypt Game

The Discovery of Egypt

NOT LONG AGO IN A LARGE UNIVERSITY TOWN IN California, on a street called Orchard Avenue, a strange old man ran a dusty shabby store. Above the dirty show windows a faded peeling sign said:

A–Z
ANTIQUES
CURIOS
USED MERCHANDISE

Nobody knew for sure what the A–Z meant. Perhaps it referred to the fact that all sorts of strange things—everything from A to Z—were sold in the store. Or perhaps it had something to do with the owner's name. However, no one seemed to know for sure what his name actually was. It was all part of a mysterious uncertainty about even the smallest item of public information about the old man. Nobody seemed certain, for instance, just why he was known as the Professor.

The neighborhood surrounding the Professor's store was made up of inexpensive apartment houses, little family-owned shops, and small, aging homes. The people of the area, many of whom had some connection with the university, could trace their ancestors to every continent, and just about every country in the world.

There were dozens of children in the neighborhood; boys and girls of every size and style and color, some of whom could speak more than one language when they wanted to. But in their schools and on the streets they all seemed to speak the same language and to have a number of things in common. And one of the things they had in common, at that time, was a vague and mysterious fear of the old man called the Professor.

Just what was so dangerous about the Professor was uncertain, like everything else about him, but his appearance undoubtedly had something to do with the rumors. He was tall and bent and his thin beard straggled up his cheeks like dry moss on gray rocks. His eyes were dark and expressionless, and set so deep under heavy brows that from a distance they looked like dark empty holes. And from a distance was the

4

only way that most of the children of Orchard Avenue cared to see them. The Professor lived somewhere at the back of his dingy store, and when he came out to stand in the sun in his doorway, smaller children would cross the street if they had to walk by.

Now and then, older and braver boys, inspired by the old man's strangeness, would dare each other into an attempt to tease or torment him—but not for long. Their absolute failure to get any sort of a reaction from their victim was not only discouraging, it was weird enough to spoil the fun for even the bravest of bullies.

Since there were several antique stores in the area to draw the buyers, the Professor seemed to do a fairly good business with out-of-town collectors; but his local trade was very small. It was said that he sold items that were used, but not antique, very cheaply, but even for grown-ups the prospect of a bargain was often not enough to offset the discomfort of the old man's stony stare.

It was one day early in a recent September that the Professor happened to be the only witness to the very beginning of the Egypt Game. He had been looking for something in a seldom used storeroom at the back of his shop, when a slight noise drew him to a window. He lifted a gunnysack curtain, rubbed a peephole in the thick coating of dirt, and peered through. Outside that particular window was a small storage

5

yard surrounded by a high board fence. It had been years since the Professor had made any use of the area, and the weed-grown yard and open lean-to shed were empty except for a few pieces of forgotten junk. But as the old man peered through his dirty window, two girls were pulling a much smaller boy through a hole in the fence.

The Professor had seen both of the girls before. They were about the same age and size, perhaps eleven or twelve years old. The one who was tugging at the little boy's leg was thin and palely blond, and her hair was arranged in a straggly pile on the top of her head. Her high cheekbones and short nose were faintly spattered with freckles and there was a strange droopy look to her eyes. The old man recalled that she had been in his store not long before, and along with some other improbable information she had disclosed that her name was April.

The other girl, who had the little boy by the shoulders, was African American, as was the little boy himself. A similarity in their pert features and slender arching eyebrows indicated that they were probably brother and sister. The Professor had seen them pass his store many times and knew that they were residents of the neighborhood.

The fence that surrounded the storage yard was high and strong and topped by strands of barbed wire, but one thin plank had come loose so that it was possible to swing it to one side. Both the girls were very slender and they had apparently squeezed through without much trouble, but the boy was causing a problem. He was only about four years old but he was sturdily built; moreover, he was clutching a large stuffed toy to his chest with both arms. He paid not the slightest attention to the demands of the two girls that he, "Turn loose of that thing for just a minute, can't you?" and, "Let me hold Security for you just till you get through, Marshall." Marshall remained very calm and patient, but his grip on his toy didn't relax for a second.

When the little boy and his huge plush octopus at last popped free into the yard, the girls turned to inspect their discovery. Their eyes flew over the broken birdbath, the crumbling statue of Diana the Huntress, and the stack of fancy wooden porch pillars, and came to rest on something in the lean-to shack. It was a cracked and chipped plaster reproduction of the famous bust of Nefertiti. The two girls stared at it for a long breathless moment and then they turned and looked at each other. They didn't say a word, but with widening eyes and small taut smiles they sent a charge of excitement dancing between them like a crackle of electricity.

The customer, an antique dealer from San Fran-

cisco, was stirring restlessly in the main room of the
store. Hearing him, the Professor was reminded of
his errand. He replaced the sacking curtain and left
the storeroom. It was more than an hour later that he
remembered the children and returned to the peephole in the dirty window.

There had been some changes made in the storage
yard. Some of the ornate old porch pillars had been
propped up around the lean-to so that they seemed to
be supporting its sagging tin roof; the statue of Diana
had been moved into position near this improvised
temple; and in the place of honor at the back and
center of the shed, the bust of Nefertiti was en-
throned in the broken birdbath. The little boy was
playing quietly with his octopus on the floor of the
shed and the two girls were busily pulling the tall dry
weeds that choked the yard, and stacking them in a
pile near the fence.

"Look, Melanie," the girl named April said. She
displayed a prickly bouquet of thistle blossoms.

"Neat!" Melanie nodded enthusiastically. "Lotus
blossoms?"

April considered her uninviting bouquet with new
appreciation. "Yeah," she agreed. "Lotus blossoms."

Melanie had another inspiration. She stood up,
dumping her lap full of weeds, and reached for the
blossoms—gingerly because of the prickles. Holding

8

them at arm's length, she announced dramatically, "The Sacred Flower of Egypt." Then she paced with dignity to the birdbath and with a curtsy presented them to Nefertiti.

April had followed, watching approvingly, but now she suddenly objected. "No! Like this," she said.

Taking the thistle flowers, she dropped to her knees and bent low before the birdbath. Then she crawled backward out of the lean-to. "Neat," Melanie said, and, taking the flowers back, she repeated the ritual, adding another refinement by tapping her forehead to the floor three times. April gave her stamp of approval to this latest innovation by trying it out herself, doing the forehead taps very slowly and dramatically. Then the two girls went back to their weed pulling, leaving the thistles before the altar of Nefertiti.

A few moments later the blond girl sat back suddenly on her heels and clapped a hand to her right eye. When she took it away the Professor, peering through his spy hole, noticed that the eye had lost its strange droopy appearance. "Melanie," April said. "They're gone. I've lost my eyelashes."

At about that point, a customer, entering the Professor's store, forced him to leave his vantage point at the dirty window. So he missed the frantic search that followed. He also missed the indignant scolding when the girls discovered that April's false eyelashes had fallen before the altar of Nefertiti, where Marshall had found them and quietly beautified one of the button eyes of his octopus.

When the Professor finally was free to return to his peephole the children had gone home, leaving the storage yard almost free from weeds, and a thistle blossom offering before the birdbath.

Enter April

HER NAME WAS APRIL HALL, BUT SHE OFTEN CALLED herself April Dawn. Exactly one month before the Egypt Game began in the Professor's backyard she had come, very reluctantly, to live in the shabby splendor of an old California-Spanish apartment house called the Casa Rosada. She came because she had been sent away by Dorothea, her beautiful and glamorous mother, to live with a grandmother she hardly knew, and who wore her gray hair in a bun on the back of her head. None of April and Dorothea's Hollywood friends ever had gray hair, except the kind you have on purpose, no matter how old they got otherwise.

It had been on that very first day, early in August, that April and the Professor first met. On that first morning of her new life April had spent half an hour

11

arranging her limp blond hair in a high upsweep, such
as Dorothea sometimes wore. It was hard work, much
harder than it looked when Dorothea did it. As she
pinned and repinned, April told herself with righteous
bitterness that Caroline was sure to make her take it
all down again anyway, and all her hard work would be
for nothing.

But if her grandmother noticed the hairdo, she said
nothing about it at the breakfast table. She didn't
even seem to notice how quiet and depressed April
was and try to cheer her up with questions and conversation. April decided that Caroline must be the
uninterested kind of person who didn't notice much
of anything. Well, that was good. Because, for the
short while she was here, April intended to go right
on leading the kind of life she was used to, and if
Caroline didn't even notice—well, at least there
wouldn't be any trouble. All through breakfast Caroline went on saying almost nothing, but finally when
she was almost through she did say that she wouldn't
mind being called Grandma or even Grannie, if
April liked.

"Oh, I guess I'll just go on calling you Caroline,"
April said. And then with pointed sweetness she
added, "That is, unless you'd rather I didn't." Dorothea always called her Caroline instead of Mother, so
what was wrong with Caroline instead of Grand-

mother? Of course, Caroline wasn't Dorothea's mother. She was the mother of April's father, who had died in an accident before April even had a chance to get to know him.

Nothing more was said until Caroline began to clear the table. Then she said, "I've arranged for you to have lunch with Mrs. Ross and her children on the second floor. She said she'd send Melanie, her little girl, up for you about twelve o'clock. The rest of the time you'll be more or less on your own, but I'd appreciate it if you'd let Mrs. Ross know if you leave the building. Just tell her where you're going and how soon you'll be back."

"I could get my own lunch," April said. "I cooked a lot at home."

"I know," Caroline said, "but I've made this arrangement with Mrs. Ross, so we'll try it for a while, just till school starts. The Rosses are very nice people. Mrs. Ross teaches school and her husband is a graduate student at the university. Their little girl is about your age, and they have a boy about four. They're African Americans," she added.

April shrugged. "Dorothea and I know a lot of black people. There are a lot of black people in show business."

Caroline smiled. "I see," she said. "Tell me, April, what do you think of the Casa Rosada?"

"The what?" April said.

"The Casa Rosada, this apartment house."

"Oh." April repeated her shrug. "It's okay." Actually it had been a pleasant surprise—that is, it would have been if she'd been in the mood for pleasant surprises. The last time she'd visited Caroline, she'd lived in a tiny supermodern apartment, like a cell, only with paintings. The Casa Rosada was very different. Somehow it made April think of Hollywood and home. It was very Spanishy-looking with great thick walls, arched doorways, fancy iron grillwork, stained-glass panels in the windows and tile floors in the lobby. Outside it was painted pink.

Caroline smiled her small prim smile. "Mr. Ross calls it the Petrified Birthday Cake, and I'm afraid that's a pretty good description. It must have been quite the thing when it was built back in the twenties. Of course, it's terribly run down now, but the apartments are roomy. It's so hard to find a modern place with two bedrooms that's not awfully expensive."

It hadn't occurred to April that Caroline had moved because of her—so she could have a bedroom of her own. She knew she ought to feel grateful, but for some reason what she really felt was angry. What made Caroline think that April was going to be with her long enough for it to make any difference whether she had a room of her own or not? Dorothea had promised it would only be for a little while. Only until

14

things got more settled down and she wasn't on tour so much of the time.

Before Caroline left she wrote down the phone number of the library at the university, where she worked, in case there was an emergency and April needed her. There wasn't much likelihood of that. April was used to taking care of herself.

When she was alone April went out on the tiny iron balcony and looked around. Caroline's apartment was on the third and top floor and fronted on the avenue. Most of the buildings in the neighborhood were only one or two stories high, so from where she stood she could get a pretty good idea of the lay of the land. On one side of the Casa Rosada were some small shops—a florist, a doughnut shop and some others. On the other, across a narrow alley, was a tall billboard that pretty much blocked the view, but by leaning forward April could see the façade of a long low building. She could tell that it was very dingy and the windows were badly in need of washing. From her position—high and to one side—she couldn't make out the sign; but from the interesting clutter in the show windows it seemed to be some sort of second-hand store.

A store of that type always offered an interesting possibility for exploring, but April was really looking for something else at the moment. A drugstore might do or perhaps a beauty shop. When Dorothea and

Nick, Dorothea's agent and good friend, had put April on the bus the morning before, they had each slipped her some money. It added up to quite a bit more than April was used to having all at once, and she wanted to make some purchases before Caroline found out about it. Not that she really thought that Caroline would take the money away, but it would be just like a grandmother to insist that it be spent on something "sensible" like new shoes or a school dress.

A few minutes later April was taking the old-fashioned elevator, with its door like a folding iron fence, down to the lobby. It wasn't until she was out on the sidewalk that she remembered what Caroline had said about reporting to Mrs. Ross before she left the building. She paused long enough to decide that reporting wouldn't be possible until that afternoon. After all, Caroline hadn't even told her where the Rosses lived, at least not exactly. With that settled to her satisfaction she went on up the street.

The girl in the drugstore looked surprised, but she didn't make too much of a big deal out of April's purchases. When she got out the false eyelashes, she did ask if they were to be a present for someone. But when April made her smile poisonously sweet and said, "Oh no," she seemed to get the point and stopped asking questions. On the way home April decided that since there was still plenty of time before twelve o'clock, she might as well explore the store she had seen from the balcony.

The store was called A–Z, and its dusty show windows were crammed with a weird clutter of old and exotic-looking objects—huge bronze oriental vases next to some beat-up old pots and pans. An old-fashioned crank telephone, a primitive-looking wooden mask and a treadle sewing machine. Two kerosene lamps and a huge broad-bladed knife with a carved ivory handle. April felt a tiny tingle of excitement. She always felt that way about old stuff. It had been one of the few things that she and Dorothea didn't agree on. Dorothea always said, "I'll take mine new and shiny."

It was dusky inside the store after the outdoor brightness. There didn't seem to be any clerks at all. Not that it mattered, because April was only looking. She squatted down in front of a glass case full of small objects: vases and jars, some partly cracked or broken, crudely made jewelry and tiny statues. All of it looked terribly ancient and interesting. She was pressing her nose to the glass when suddenly she knew she was being watched.

An old man was leaning over the counter right above her head. "Oh hello," April said and went on looking at a tiny statue with broad shoulders, short legs and a hole in the top of its head. It looked almost Egyptian and April had always been especially inter-

ested in Egyptian stuff. After a moment she looked up
again and the man was still there. "What's that?"
she asked, pointing to the tiny figure.

"That is a pre-Columbian burial figure. It was made
in Mexico about two thousand years ago." The old
man's voice was slow and rusty.

April looked up again quickly. "Two thousand—
you're kidding," she said. But on second glance she
was sure he wasn't. He wasn't kidding and he wasn't
quite like anyone she'd ever seen before. He had a

strange skimpy-looking little beard and his eyes were deep set and as blank as an empty well. He said nothing more, and not by so much as a flicker did his face reveal what he was thinking.

April was impressed. A deadpan was something she'd cultivated herself, and she knew from experience that such a perfect one was not easily come by. "I mean," she said with respectful caution, "is it really that old?"

The old man only tilted his stone face downward

in a stiff nod. April went back to studying the objects in the case, but now her interest was divided. The old man was almost as unusual as the strange things behind the dusty glass. In a few moments she stood up and smiled at him. It was a real smile, small and quick, not the gooey kind she usually used on grownups. Somehow she had a notion he wouldn't fool easily.

"My name is April Hall," she said. "I've just come to live in the apartment house next door, with my grandmother. I used to live in Hollywood with my mother." She paused. For a moment it looked as if the old man wasn't going to answer at all, but at last his craggy face cracked enough to allow the escape of two small words, "I see."

April regarded him with grudging admiration. It usually wasn't very hard to pick the real meaning out of things people said, if you watched them closely. But this one wasn't going to be easy. The "I see" said nothing at all. It wasn't friendly, or angry, or curious, or even bored. In fact, there was something about the absolute nothingness behind it that was a little bit frightening, like putting out your hand to touch something that wasn't really there. April began to chatter a little nervously. "I'm a nut about things like that." She motioned towards the case. "I'm always reading about ancient times and stuff like that. You know, Babylonia and Egypt and Greece and China.

It's kind of a hobby of mine. As a matter of fact, I'm even planning to be an archaeologist when I grow up. Some people think that's a pretty kooky ambition for a girl—but I like it. You see, I have this theory about how I was a high priestess once, in an earlier reincarnation. Do you think that's possible?"

"Possible?" The old man's voice quavered the word into a whole flock of syllables. "Many things are possible."

"That's what I think, too. A lot of people don't think so, though. When I told Nick—he's my mother's agent—about the high priestess thing he just laughed. He said, 'I don't know about those other reincarnations, kiddo, but in this one you're a nut.' "

Before the old man could answer, if he was going to, a couple of ladies breezed in the doorway. Of course, they interrupted right away when they saw that April was just a kid.

As she drifted out the door and back to the Casa Rosada, April wondered why she'd gabbed so much. It wasn't really like her. She'd started out just trying to get the old man to talk and then somehow she couldn't quit. It was almost as if the old man's deadly silence was a dangerous dark hole that had to be filled up quickly with lots of words.

Enter Melanie—and Marshall

On that same day in August, just a few minutes before twelve, Melanie Ross arrived at the door of Mrs. Hall's apartment on the third floor. Melanie was eleven years old and she had lived in the Casa Rosada since she was only seven. During that time she'd welcomed a lot of new people to the apartment house. Apartment dwellers, particularly near a university, are apt to come and go. Melanie always looked forward to meeting new tenants, and today was going to be especially interesting. Today, Melanie had been sent up to get Mrs. Hall's granddaughter to come down and have lunch with the Rosses. Melanie didn't know much about the new girl except that her name was April and that she had come from Hollywood to live with Mrs. Hall, who was her grandmother.

It would be neat if she turned out to be a real

friend. There hadn't been any girls the right age in the Casa Rosada lately. To have a handy friend again, for spur-of-the-moment visiting, would be great. However, she had overheard something that didn't sound too promising. Just the other day she'd heard Mrs. Hall telling Mom that April was a strange little thing because she'd been brought up all over everywhere and never had much of a chance to associate with other children. You wouldn't know what to expect of someone like that. But then, you never knew what to expect of any new kid, not really. So Melanie knocked hopefully at the door of apartment 312.

Meeting people had always been easy for Melanie. Most people she liked right away, and they usually seemed to feel the same way about her. But when the door to 312 opened that morning, for just a moment she was almost speechless. Surprise can do that to a person, and at first glance April really was a surprise. Her hair was stacked up in a pile that seemed to be more pins than hair, and the whole thing teetered forward over her thin pale face. She was wearing a big, yellowish-white fur thing around her shoulders, and carrying a plastic purse almost as big as a suitcase. But most of all it was the eyelashes. They were black and bushy looking, and the ones on her left eye were higher up and sloped in a different direction. Melanie's mouth opened and closed a few times before anything came out.

April adjusted Dorothea's old fur stole, patted up some sliding strands of hair and waited—warily. She didn't expect this Melanie to like her—kids hardly ever did—but she *did* intend to make a very definite impression; and she could see that she'd done that all right.

"Hi," Melanie managed after that first speechless moment. "I'm Melanie Ross. You're supposed to have lunch with us, I think. Aren't you April Hall?"

"April Dawn," April corrected with an offhand sort of smile. "I was expecting you. My grandmother informed me that—uh, she said you'd be up."

It occurred to Melanie that maybe kids dressed differently in Hollywood. As they started down the hall she asked, "Are you going to stay with your grandmother for very long?"

"Oh no," April said. "Just till my mother finishes this tour she's on. Then she'll send for me to come home."

"Tour?"

"Yes, you see my mother is Dorothea Dawn—" she paused and Melanie racked her brain. She could tell she was supposed to know who Dorothea Dawn was. "Well, I guess you haven't happened to hear of her way up here, but she's a singer and in the movies, and stuff like that. But right now she's singing with this band that travels around to different places."

"Neat!" Melanie said. "You mean your mother's in the movies?"

But just then they arrived at the Rosses' apartment. Marshall met them at the door, dragging Security by one of his eight legs.

"That's my brother, Marshall," Melanie said.

"Hi, Marshall," April said. "Hey, what's that following you, kid?"

Melanie grinned. "That's Security. Marshall takes him everywhere. So my dad named him Security. You know. Like some little kids have a blanket."

"Security's an octopus," Marshall said very clearly. He didn't talk very much, but when he did he always said exactly what he wanted to without any trouble. He never had fooled around with baby talk.

Melanie's mother was in the kitchen putting hot dog sandwiches and fruit salad on the table. When Melanie introduced April she could tell that her mother was surprised by the eyelashes and hairdo and everything. She probably didn't realize that kids dressed a little differently in Hollywood.

"April's mother is a movie star," Melanie explained.

Melanie's mother smiled. "Is that right, April?" she asked.

April looked at Melanie's mother carefully through narrowed eyes. Mrs. Ross looked sharp and neat, with a smart-looking very short hairdo like a soft black cap, and high winging eyebrows, like Melanie's. But her smile was a little different. April was good at figuring out what adults meant by the things they didn't quite say—and Mrs. Ross's smile meant that she wasn't going to be easy to snow.

"Well," April admitted, "not a star, really. She's mostly a vocalist. So far she's only been an extra in the movies. But she almost had a supporting role once, and Nick, that's her agent, says he has a big part almost all lined up."

"Wow, that's cool!" Melanie said. "We've never known anyone before whose mother was an extra in the movies, have we, Mom?"

"Not a soul," Mrs. Ross said, still smiling.

During lunch, April talked a lot about Hollywood, and the movie stars she'd met and the big parties her mother gave and things like that. She knew she was overdoing it a bit but something made her keep on. Mrs. Ross went right on smiling in that knowing way, and Melanie went right on being so eager and encouraging that April thought she must be kidding. She wasn't sure, though. You never could tell with kids—they didn't do things in a pattern, the way grown-ups did.

Actually Melanie knew that April was showboating, but it occurred to her that it was probably because of homesickness. It was easy to see how much she'd like to be back in Hollywood with her mother.

While they were having dessert of ice cream and

cookies, Mrs. Ross suggested that April might like to look over Melanie's books to see if there was anything she'd like to borrow.

"Do you like to read?" Melanie asked. "Reading is my favorite occupation."

"That's for sure." Mrs. Ross laughed. "A full-time occupation with overtime. Your grandmother tells me that you do a lot of reading, too."

"Well, of course, I'm usually pretty busy, with all the parties and everything. I do read some, though, when I have a chance."

But after lunch when Melanie showed April her library, a whole bookcase full in her bedroom, she could tell that April liked books more than just a little. She could tell just by the way April picked a book up and handled it, and by the way she forgot about acting so grown-up and Hollywoodish. She plopped herself down on the floor in front of the bookcase and started looking at books like crazy. For a while she seemed to forget all about Melanie. As she read she kept propping up her eyelashes with one finger.

All of a sudden she said, "Could you help me get these stupid things off? I must not have put them on the right place or something. When I look down to read I can't even see the words."

So Melanie scratched the ends of the eyelashes

loose with her longest fingernail, and then April pulled them the rest of the way off. They were on pretty tight, and she said, "Ouch!" several times and a couple of other words that Melanie wasn't allowed to say.

"—— ——!" said April, looking in the mirror. "I think I pulled out most of my real ones. Does it look like it to you?"

"I don't think so," Melanie said. "I still see some. Is this the first time you've worn them? The false ones, I mean?"

April put back on her haughty face. "Of course not. Nearly everybody wears them in Hollywood. My mother wears them all the time. It's just that these are new ones, and they must be a different kind."

April put her eyelashes away carefully in her big bag and they went back to looking at books. Melanie showed her some of her favorites, and April picked out a couple to borrow. It was then that April took a very special book off the shelf.

It was a very dull-looking old geography book that no one would be interested in. That was why Melanie used it to hide something very special and secret. As April opened the book some cutout paper people fell out on the floor.

"What are those?" April asked.

"Just some old things of mine," Melanie said,

holding out her hand for the book, but April kept on turning the pages and finding more bunches of paper people.

"Do you really still play with paper dolls?" April asked in just the tone of voice that Melanie had feared she would use. Not just because she was April, either. It was the tone of voice that nearly anyone would use about a sixth-grade girl who still played with ordinary paper dolls.

"But they're not really paper dolls," Melanie said, "and I don't really play with them. Not like moving them around and dressing them up and everything. They're just sort of a record for a game I play. I make up a family and then I find people who look like them in magazines and catalogues. Just so I'll remember them better. I have fourteen families now. See, they all have their names and ages written on the back. I make up stuff about their personalities and what they do. Sometimes I write it down like a story, but usually I just make it up."

April's scornful look was dissolving. "Like what?"

"Well," Melanie said, "this is the Brewster family. Mr. Brewster is a detective. I had to cut him out of the newspaper because he was the only man I could find who looked like a detective. Don't you think he does?"

"Yeah, pretty much."

"Well anyway, he just—that is, I just made up

about how he solved this very hard mystery and caught some dangerous criminals. And then the criminals escaped and were going to get revenge on Mr. Brewster. So the whole family had to go into hiding and wear disguises and everything."

April spread the Brewsters out on the floor. Her eyes were shining and without the eyelashes they were pretty, wide and blue. "Have they caught the criminals yet?" she asked. Melanie shook her head. "Well, how about if the kids catch them. They could just happen to find out where the criminals were hiding?"

"Neat!" Melanie said. "Maybe Ted"—she pointed to the smallest paper Brewster—"could come home and tell the other kids how he thinks he saw one of the criminals, going into a certain house."

"And then," April interrupted, "the girls could go to the house pretending to sell Girl Scout cookies, to see if it really was the crooks."

From the Girl-Scout-cookies caper, the game moved into even more exciting escapades, and when Mrs. Ross came in to say that Marshall was down for his nap and that she was leaving for the university, where she was taking a summer course for schoolteachers, the criminals were just escaping, taking one of the Brewster children with them as a hostage. An hour later, when Marshall came in sleepy-eyed and dragging Security, several of the other paper families had been brought into the plot. Marshall seemed

31

content to sit and listen, so the game went on with daring adventures, narrow escapes, tragic illnesses and even a romance or two. At last, right in the middle of a shipwreck on a desert island, April noticed the time and said she'd have to go home so she'd be there when Caroline got back from work.

As they walked to the door Melanie asked, "Do you want to play some more tomorrow?"

April was adjusting her fur stole around her shoulders for the trip upstairs. "Oh, I guess so," she said with a sudden return to haughtiness.

But Melanie was beginning to understand about April's frozen spells, and how to thaw her out. You just had to let her know she couldn't make you stop liking her that easily. "None of my friends know how to play imagining games the way you do," Melanie said. "Some of them can do it a little bit but they mostly don't have any very good ideas. And a lot of them only like ball games or other things that are already made up. But I like imagining games better than anything."

April was being very busy trying to get her stole to stay on because the clasp was a little bit broken. All at once she pulled it off, wadded it all up and tucked it under her arm. She looked right straight at Melanie and said, "You know what? I never did call them that before, but imagining games are just about all I ever play because most of the time I never have anybody to play with."

She started off up the hall. Then she turned around and walked backward, waving her fur stole around her head like a lasso. "You've got lots of good ideas, too," she yelled.

The Egypt Girls

ALL THROUGH THE MONTH OF AUGUST, MELANIE AND April were together almost every day. They played the paper-families game and other games, both in the Rosses' apartment and in Caroline's. They took Marshall for walks and to the park while Mrs. Ross was gone to her class, and almost every day they went to the library. It was in the library in August that the seeds were planted that grew into the Egypt Game in September in the Professor's deserted yard.

It all started when April found a new book about Egypt, an especially interesting one about the life of a young pharaoh. She passed it on to Melanie, and with it a lot of her interest in all sorts of ancient stuff. Melanie was soon as fascinated by the valley of the Nile as April had been. Before long, with the help of a sympathetic librarian, they had found and read

just about everything the library had to offer on Egypt
—both fact and fiction.

They read about Egypt in the library during the
day, and at home in the evening, and in bed late at
night when they were supposed to be asleep. Then in
the mornings while they helped each other with their
chores they discussed the things they had found out.
In a very short time they had accumulated all sorts of
fascinating facts about tombs and temples, pharaohs
and pyramids, mummies and monoliths, and dozens
of other exotic topics. They decided that the Egyptians couldn't have been more interesting if they had
done it on purpose. Everything, from their love of
beauty and mystery, to their fascinating habit of getting married when they were only eleven years old,
made good stuff to talk about. By the end of the
month, April and Melanie were beginning work on
their own alphabet of hieroglyphics for writing secret
messages, and at the library they were beginning to be
called the Egypt Girls.

But in between all the good times, both April and
Melanie were spending some bad moments worrying
about the beginning of school. April was worried because she knew from experience—lots of it—that it
isn't easy to face a new class in a new school. She
didn't admit it, not even to Melanie, but she was having nightmares about the first day of school. There
were classroom nightmares, and schoolyard night-

mares and principal's office nightmares; but there was another kind, too, that had to do with an empty mailbox. In the whole month of August she had had only one very short postcard from Dorothea.

Melanie was worried, too, but in a different way. School had always been easy for Melanie; and even though she wasn't the kind who got elected class president, she'd always had plenty of friends. But now there was April to think about.

April was the most exciting friend Melanie had ever had. No one else knew about so many fascinating things, or could think up such marvelous things to do. With April, a walk to the library could become an exploration of a forbidden land, or a shiny pebble on the sidewalk could be a magic token from an invisible power. When April got that imagining gleam in her eye there was no telling what was going to happen next. Just about any interesting subject you could mention, April was sure to know a lot of weird and wonderful facts about it. And if she didn't, you could always count on her to make up a few, just to keep things going.

There was only one thing that April didn't seem to know much about—that was getting along with people. Most people, anyhow. With Melanie, April was herself, new and different from anyone, wild and daring and terribly brave. But with other people she was often quite different. With other kids she usually put on her Hollywood act, terribly grown-up and bored with everything. And with most grown-ups April's eyes got narrow and you couldn't believe a word she said.

Melanie had gone to Wilson School all her life, and she knew what it was like. There were all different kinds of kids at Wilson; kids who looked and talked and acted all sorts of ways. Wilson was used to that. But there were some things that Wilson kids just wouldn't stand for, and Melanie was afraid that April's Hollywood act was one of them.

And Melanie wasn't entirely just guessing about how her schoolmates would react to April. A couple of times when April and Melanie had been at the library or in the park they'd run into some of the Wilson kids Melanie knew; and you could see right away that April wasn't making the right kind of impression. And it was going to be worse at school, where every kid would feel duty bound to do his or her part in trimming the new kid down to size. Melanie had a feeling that April wasn't going to trim easily.

The thing that worried Melanie the most was the eyelashes. April was still wearing them a lot of the time. She'd gotten so she didn't wear them to the library because she still had trouble reading through them, but even if she hadn't had them on all day she always put them on when it was time for her grandmother to come home. Once Melanie asked her why.

"She doesn't like for me to wear them," April said.

Melanie thought about that for a minute. Then she said, "You don't like your grandmother very much, do you?"

April just shrugged but her eyes got narrow.

"I don't see why," Melanie said. "She seems pretty nice to me."

"She doesn't like my mother," April said. "She doesn't even think that Dorothea's going to send for me to come home pretty soon."

"Did she say so?"

"No, but she thinks it. I can tell."

Then, just at the beginning of September, with school only a few days away, came that exciting day when the Egypt Game began. April and Melanie and Marshall were on their way home through the alley when, by the sheerest luck, Melanie noticed the loose plank. It had moved stiffly, that first time, with a reluctant rusty yelp and they peeked through into the hidden and deserted yard. It was fascinating—so weed-grown and forgotten and secret—but then came the most unbelievably wonderful part of all.

There she was, waiting for them in the shed, Nefertiti, the beautiful queen of ancient Egypt, like a magical omen, or, as April put it, "a beautiful messenger from out of the ancient past." There had to be something terribly out-of-the-ordinary about it. Why, it had only been a few days before that they had read

38

all about her and admired a picture of her lovely sculptured head. And there it was, almost like magic. Very much like magic, in fact—and that's the way the Egypt Game was, from the very beginning.

But even the discovery of Egypt didn't stop the beginning of school from arriving with all its problems. So, when April lost one of her eyelashes that first day in Egypt, Melanie couldn't help feeling a little relieved, although she wouldn't have said so. But then, there it was on Security—and the problem was just as complicated as ever. It was the next morning when Melanie finally got up nerve enough to talk to April about it.

April was helping Melanie dry the dishes so they'd be ready to leave for Egypt sooner. "Are you going to wear your eyelashes to school?" Melanie asked with careful casualness.

But April turned quickly, and with her face all shut up the way it was with other people. "Sure," she said. "Why not?"

"Oh, I don't know. I just don't think anybody else at Wilson wears them."

April's chin went up and her lips thinned. "Am I supposed to care what the kids at a little old place like Wilson School wear?"

Melanie could see that she wasn't going to get anywhere so she let the subject drop. But before the dishes were finished she had started making a drastic plan. April just couldn't wear those eyelashes to school on the first day. She was going to be hard enough to integrate even without them.

As soon as Melanie had finished her chores they were free to head for Egypt. Since it was Saturday, Melanie's parents were both at home, but Mr. Ross always had to study and he was only too glad for the girls to get Marshall out from underfoot. Just outside the apartment door April stopped with her finger to her lips.

"Shhh," she warned, "we must proceed with caution. We may be being watched."

"Who's watching?" Marshall asked, looking around.

"The enemies of Egypt. Who were those worst enemies, Melanie?"

"The Syrians," Melanie whispered.

"Yeah, they're the ones. The Syrians. Their spies are everywhere."

With elaborate caution they made their way out of the back door of the Casa Rosada and down the alley. They went the wrong way first and took evasive action through a garage and around a stack of garbage pails. Then they crawled through a piece of cement pipe and started to make a run for it; but they had to go back for Marshall, who was still in the pipe, all tangled up in Security's legs. When they finally arrived at the fence they were out of breath.

"All clear?" Melanie asked, looking both ways.

"Yes, for the time being," April breathed. "But they almost had us. That was a close call back there in the tunnel."

"Close," Melanie agreed, "but we fooled them." With that they shoved Marshall through the hole in the fence and crawled in after him.

The Evil God
and the Secret Spy

WHEN APRIL AND MARSHALL AND MELANIE SQUEEZED back through the fence for the second time they found everything just as they had left it. They started out by pulling the rest of the dead weeds and stacking them in one corner of the yard. While Marshall stood guard halfway down the alley to see if anyone was coming, they shoved the whole stack out through the hole in the fence. Then they scouted around and found a trash bin that was nice and roomy and not too full to hold an extra donation of dead weeds. When, at last, the loose stones and broken bits of things had been cleared away, Egypt looked clean and bare and ready for whatever might be going to happen.

Next they turned their attention to the lean-to shed, or the Temple, as they were already beginning to call it. It was actually only a wooden platform about a foot off the ground, across one end of the yard. A roof of corrugated tin was supported in the front by a few wooden posts, and on the other three sides walls were formed by the tall boards of the fence. Already the birdbath altar of Nefertiti, the fancy pillars from the porch of some Victorian mansion and the crumbling statue of Diana by the entrance were beginning to create a temple-like atmosphere. But there was much more that could be done.

April and Melanie were sitting on the edge of the Temple's floor resting for a moment, and planning, when April pointed out the only real door to the storage yard. It was on the opposite site from the loose plank and was apparently locked with a latch and padlock from the outside. "I wonder where it goes to," she said.

Melanie thought a moment. "I guess it goes to the rest of the Professor's backyard," she said. "You know, that part with a driveway so trucks and things can back up to his store for deliveries. You can see into that part from the alley." It was right then when she mentioned the Professor that Melanie, for the first time, had an uncomfortable feeling. "What do you suppose the Professor would do if he caught us in here?" she wondered out loud.

April shrugged. Melanie had told her how most

of the children in the neighborhood felt about the Professor. While she had to admit he'd been a little bit creepy, she didn't see what all the fuss was about. But Melanie seemed to feel that April's short talk with the old man had made her an authority on the subject, so she was more or less obliged to come up with an opinion. "I don't think he'd do a thing," she said. "I just don't think he'd even care, as long as we don't bother him or hurt anything. Besides, how's he going to know? You can tell by the weeds and everything that no one's been in here for ages. I'll bet the padlock on that door's rusted so tight he couldn't get in if he wanted to. And that window isn't the kind that opens. He'd have to break the glass if he wanted to get through."

"He might be watching us through it, though."

Somehow that thought was almost more scary than the possibility of the Professor's actually entering the yard. With one accord the girls moved warily towards the window. Closer and closer until their noses were only inches from the dirty panes. Then Melanie breathed a sigh of relief. "There's something like a heavy curtain hanging clear across it. He couldn't see through that."

"Besides, I don't think he could see through the dirt even if there wasn't a curtain. I'll bet this window's in some little back room he doesn't even use any more. Otherwise he wouldn't leave it so dirty."

Feeling pleasantly safe and secure, the girls sat back down and began to make plans. Marshall was busy digging a little hole in the middle of the yard with a sharp stick. He had knotted two of Security's legs together around his neck so that his hands would be free for digging. Security's pear-shaped plush body and six of his black legs were hanging down Marshall's back.

"I know," April said suddenly, "Marshall can be the young pharaoh, heir to the throne of Egypt. Only there's a civil war going on, and the other side is trying to kill him."

"Okay. And we can be high priestesses of Isis who are assigned to protect him."

"Ummm," April said. "Or else we could be evil high priestesses who are going to offer him as a human sacrifice on the crocodile altar to—what was that evil god's name?"

"Set?"

"Yeah, that's the one." April jumped to her feet. Throwing up her arms, she chanted, "Almighty Set has promised his servants, the crocodile gods of the Nile, the bloody heart of the young Pharaoh, Marsh—uh, Marshamosis!" She dropped to her knees. "O mighty Set, god of evil, we hear and obey."

Marshall had stopped digging, and now he stood up and started towards the opening in the fence. The girls ran after him. He didn't struggle when they caught him, but Melanie was familiar with the ex-

pression on his face. His funny little baby-round chin was sticking out defiantly and his black eyes glared. "Leave my bloody heart alone," he said.

The girls giggled. "You know, he's pretty sharp for a four-year-old," April said.

Melanie got down on her knees and tried to take Marshall's hands, but he wouldn't turn loose of Security. "Marshall, honey," she said, "it's just a game. Just pretend. We wouldn't really hurt you."

"What's a pharaoh?" Marshall asked suspiciously.

"A king," Melanie said, "king of all the Egyptians." Marshall's frown lifted a little and his chin began to go back into its normal position.

"A terribly important kind of king," April said. "Everybody had to bow down to him and do exactly what he said."

Marshall nodded soberly. "I'll play," he said.

So that was the way Set started—Set the god of evil and black magic. At first he was just supposed to be a character in that particular game, and that first day he was represented by a picture of a man with an animal's head that Melanie drew on a piece of cardboard and tacked to the wall. But once he got started, he seemed to grow and develop almost on his own, and all out of control; until he was more than evil, and at times a lot more than Egyptian. For instance, at different times, his wicked tricks included everything from atomic ray guns to sulfur and brimstone.

But, actually, that was the way with all of the Egypt Game. Nobody ever planned it ahead, at least, not very far. Ideas began and grew and afterwards it was hard to remember just how. That was one of the mysterious and fascinating things about it.

On that particular day, the game about Marshamosis, the boy pharaoh, and Set, the god of evil, didn't get very far. They'd no more than gotten started when April and Melanie decided they just had to have some more equipment before they could play it well. So they postponed the game and went instead to scout around in the alley for boards and boxes to use in making things like thrones and altars. They found just what they needed behind the doughnut shop and the furniture store in the next block, and brought them back to Egypt. And it was on the same trip that they had the good luck to rescue an old metal mixing bowl from a garbage pail. April said it would be just the thing for a firepit for building sacred fires.

When they had everything as far as the hole in the fence, they ran into a problem. The bowl and boards went through all right, but the boxes were just too big. The only solution was to throw them over the top of the fence. It wasn't easy, and in landing they made quite a bit of noise.

It wasn't long afterwards that the curtain on the small window at the back of the Professor's store was pushed very carefully to one side. But April and Melanie were so busy building and planning that they didn't notice at all. Only someone with very sharp eyes would have been able to see the figure that stood silently behind the very dirty window in the darkened room.

Eyelashes and Ceremony

THE NEXT DAY WAS THE LAST BEFORE SCHOOL WAS TO start. It was also Melanie's last chance to put into effect her plan to get rid of the eyelashes. So after dinner she went up to Mrs. Hall's apartment to see April. She took the library book that she was reading and one that she knew April wanted to read.

In April's room they talked about the Egypt Game and about school starting in the morning—what they were going to wear and things like that. Then Melanie suggested they read for a while, so they got comfortable on their stomachs across April's bed and started in on the books—and sure enough, April got up and took off her eyelashes so she could see better.

But, for once, both the girls had a hard time keeping their minds on their reading. April was thinking about the next day, telling herself that it didn't matter whether the people at Wilson School were friendly or not, because Dorothea would write soon saying she wanted April to come home. Dorothea—it seemed ages since April had seen her. April shut her eyes and tried to picture her, but tonight the picture wouldn't come clear. It was only a blur—a blur of laughter, talk, movement and color. But a bright and beautiful blur, no matter how distant, was better than a reality that was dull and gray.

Melanie was having trouble keeping her mind on her reading because she was so worried about what she was planning to do. In fact, they both were having such a hard time pretending not to worry that they were secretly relieved when Caroline came in and suggested it was bedtime for girls who were going to school in the morning. The eyelashes were lying on April's dresser and Melanie managed to walk right past them as she went out. Because of the sticky stuff to make them stay on your eyelids, she only had to brush her hand against them to pick them up. Feeling triumphant and treacherous at the same time, Melanie took the eyelashes home and hid them in her closet. She kept them there until the first few days of school were over. Then she took them back and put them under April's dresser, so it would look as if they'd just happened to fall. By that time April had gotten out of the notion of wearing them to school.

But even without the eyelashes Melanie had a hard

time trying to translate April into something that
Wilson School could understand and appreciate. April
was still wearing her hair in a messy upsweep and her
mother's ratty old fur stole, even though her grandmother had given her a great new jacket. Besides, she
still put on her Hollywood act with people she didn't
know, and worst of all, she got furiously angry when
she was teased. Melanie could see that to the kids at
Wilson, all the stuff April knew made her a know-it-
all; her wonderful differentness was only kookiness;
and her courage only meant she'd punch you in the
nose if you kidded her, no matter how many teachers
were looking.

At least, that was the way it was for a while. But
with Melanie working her hardest as go-between, it
wasn't too long before things began to be a little better. The sixth grade began to find out that April had a
way of making life interesting. For instance, when she
raised her hand in class, her answer wasn't always
what the teacher wanted, but it was almost certain to
be fascinating. And when it came to guts—whether it
was hanging by your heels from the highest bar, or
putting a stinkbug on the principal's desk—you could
count on April to do it first and best.

By the third week in September, although the sixth
graders were still teasing April—from a safe distance
—they were beginning to think of her rather proudly,
as their own private oddball. But it was when Toby

and Ken gave her a nickname that Melanie knew for sure that the worst was over. Toby Alvillar and Ken Kamata were two of the biggest wheels in class, and if you were really hopeless they simply didn't notice you —it was as if you didn't exist. So when they started calling April, February, Melanie knew everything would be all right. It was teasing, maybe, but not the kind you use on outsiders.

In the meantime, in the afternoons and on weekends, the Egypt Game was really beginning to take shape. As soon as school was out every day, the girls picked up Marshall at his nursery school and hurried home. Then they were free to spend their time in Egypt, until almost 5:30, when Caroline and the Rosses came home.

The lean-to temple now had two altars and two gods. The birdbath altar had been moved to the right side, while on the left was the altar of Set, the Evil One. Set's altar was made from an egg crate covered by a piece of an old bedspread, and the god himself was a rather pear-shaped figure of dried mud. April and Melanie had looked and looked for a suitable Set. For a while they tried a Chinese kitchen-god figurine from Schmitt's Variety Store, but he was all wrong—much too nice and pleasant looking. At last, they had to resort to making a Set themselves, from some clayey mud from the Casa Rosada's dead flower garden. Except for his glowing eyes, which were made of glass buttons of a deep fiery red, he didn't turn out particularly well. In fact, at first he seemed rather laughable. But as time passed and the game progressed, Set's face hardened and cracked into a wicked leer, and it became clear that his strange, sunken, formless body was the very shape of evil. Dark and deep as the mud of the Nile, Set brooded lumpily through a mist of sandalwood incense—ninety-nine cents at Schmitt's—over all kinds of mystic ceremonies, weird rites and wicked plots.

Opposite the altar of the wicked god stood the bird-bath throne of the goddess of goodness. Of course, she was still represented by the plaster bust of Nefertiti, but as the game went on she began to be called Isis most of the time, because she was a goddess and not just a queen. And since the pharaohs were supposed to be related to the gods, it really didn't matter if Isis and Nefertiti got a little bit confused. Whatever her name, what she stood for was always the same— love and beauty and every kind of perfection.

There was always a great deal to do in the land of Egypt. Right at first April and Melanie got terribly involved in composing and practicing rites and ceremonies for the two gods. The rituals were very complicated and the correct order of processions, chants, prostrations, sprinklings with holy water and sacrificial offerings had to be carefully written down so that they wouldn't be forgotten. At first the records were on ordinary notebook paper, but then Melanie, whose handwriting was the nicest, put it all down on onion-skin paper rolled on pieces of an old fishing pole they'd found in the alley. Each page was glued on two pieces of pole so it could be rolled and unrolled like a papyrus scroll. Someday, they decided, they would do it all over in hieroglyphics, when they'd found time to finish their hieroglyphic alphabet, but for the present it was just written in English. Then, when Marshall discovered that the wooden base of the Diana statue was hollow, and one side was a little loose, they had a perfect secret vault for the storage of sacred records.

Of course the temple and the two altars had to be decorated, too. It wasn't at all difficult to find the right sort of things for the altar of Nefertiti-Isis. Flowers, candles, beads, pretty stones, blown-glass figurines of birds and deer, in fact, anything beautiful, seemed to suit the lovely goddess. One day Melanie brought her poster paints and they painted stars and birds and flowers on the fence in back of the altar; and another day they made a canopy to hang above Nefertiti's head. They made it from an old fluffy half-slip of crinoline and lace, but when they were through cutting and pinning and tacking, it looked exactly like a canopy and not like a petticoat at all.

Set was more of a problem. For a while he had

only his incense burner, which was made of an old metal ash tray. April suggested that they might find something suitable in the Professor's store, but Melanie wouldn't go with her to help her shop. Melanie had lived too long in the neighborhood and been almost brought up on all those scary rumors about the Professor. And besides, she said, what could they buy for fifty cents, which was about all they could scrape up at the time. So Set had to settle for some spiders and snakes painted on the wall behind him, and a dry bone that hung on a string above his head. April had gone to the trouble of tricking an unfriendly dog out of the bone because it was so large and sinister looking; and it had just the right effect hanging there over the evil god, twisting and turning in the wind.

Then one day on the way to school Melanie found a strange dark stone. It was lying in the middle of a sidewalk, where a stone had no reason to be; but even more mysterious, when you held it at just the right angle it looked exactly like a pair of long pointed jaws with a bulging snout and jagged teeth.

"There's no doubt about it," April said, "it's no ordinary rock, that's for sure."

So they put it on the altar, too, and called it the Crocodile Stone, and from then on it became the mysterious and powerful source of much of Set's power.

At first Marshall only watched everything that was going on, but after a while he began to be impatient and wanted to know, "When are you going to play about the pharaoh some more, like you said?" When April told him they wouldn't be ready for that for a long time, his chin began to stick out. So, to keep him happy, they let him start being a sort of junior high priest. At the next ceremony, which was to be the presentation of a dead lizard as a sacrificial offering to Set, Marshall marched at the head of the procession and sprinkled holy water from a tuna can. He did a good job, too, except that he wouldn't put Security down, not even to be a high priest.

At first April said nobody could be the high priest of an evil god with a toy octopus hanging around his neck, but she finally agreed they could pretend it was some kind of a fancy ceremonial robe. And when the procession was over she had to admit that Marshall had done awfully well, for a little kid. "He even remembered all the words to the chant and he sprinkled in all the right places," she said wonderingly. But Melanie wasn't surprised at all.

"That's the way with Marshall," she said. "He's been awfully grown-up ever since—oh, since about the time he started walking. That is, about everything except Security. I guess he's not very grown-up about that. Dad says the reason Marshall needs Security is that he had such a hard time being a baby. Dad says being a baby offended Marshall's dignity."

April shrugged. "Yeah, I guess everybody has something they're not very grown-up about," she said.

Neferbeth

NEAR THE END OF SEPTEMBER A NEW GIRL MOVED
into the Casa Rosada. Her name was Elizabeth
Chung. She and her mother and two little sisters had
rented the little semibasement apartment next to
where Mr. Bodler, the janitor, lived. Caroline went
down to call on Mrs. Chung the evening the family
moved in to see if there was anything she could do to
help them get settled. She asked April if she wanted
to go along to meet Elizabeth, but April said, "No
thanks."

When her grandmother came back upstairs, April
found out all about the new family. Mr. Chung had
died recently and his wife was going to have to get a
job to support her three little girls. She had moved to
the Casa Rosada because it was only a few blocks
from where her parents lived. Mrs. Chung's mother

was going to take care of the two smallest girls while she was at work.

"Elizabeth is only a little younger than you and Melanie," Caroline said. "Perhaps you could ask her to play with you. She's probably feeling lonely and worried about starting in at a new school."

April was ambushed by a quick pang of sympathy, remembering how it was—missing someone and having to face a new classroom. But she pulled herself together and shook it off. It occurred to her that Caroline ought to know that you didn't pick your friends just because they were handy—or even lonely. You picked them because you thought alike and were interested in the same things, the way she and Melanie were. "How old *is* she?" she asked, letting her eyes go narrow.

"I think her mother said she was nine," Caroline said.

"Nine," said April, with a cool smile, "is a lot younger than eleven."

"Well, of course, it will have to be up to you and Melanie to decide," Caroline said calmly, but as she turned to leave the room April was sure she heard a rather exasperated sigh.

April tried to feel pleased about the sigh, but something prickled uncomfortably. She decided she didn't want to think about it. She called to Caroline that she was going down to talk to Melanie. Melanie would understand how impossible it would be to invite someone else to be part of anything so private and secret as the Egypt Game.

Mr. Ross called, "Come in," when April knocked. He was sitting on the couch surrounded by books and papers. He was studying to be a college teacher and he always had a lot of work to do in the evenings. He was a big man with dark brown skin and a teasing smile. He was always kidding April about her name. When April opened the door he said, "Just as I thought, it's springtime. Melanie! the cruelest month is here."

Mr. Ross was going to teach things like poetry and literature, and he was always making jokes that weren't very funny unless you knew what he was talking about. That "cruelest month" business, for instance, was something he was always kidding April about. It didn't make any sense to April until Melanie found out about it and explained. It seemed it came from a big long poem that started out about how April was the "cruelest month." April still didn't think it was any riot, but she guessed it was okay for that kind of joke.

As soon as the girls were alone in Melanie's room, April brought up the subject of Elizabeth. Sure enough, Melanie's mother had been after her, too, to make the new girl feel at home.

"I don't know what they think we can do," April

said. "We can't let her in on the Egypt Game. She'd be sure to fink about it and ruin everything."

"Well, we'll have to get to know her first," Melanie said, "and see if she's the kind who can keep a secret. And then—"

"Keep a secret!" April interrupted scornfully. "For one thing, she's only nine years old."

"Well, Marshall's only four," Melanie said, "and he doesn't ever fink."

"Marshall's different," April said impatiently. "This Elizabeth is probably just like any other blabber-mouth fourth grader."

Alarmed at what seemed to her to be a rather wishy-washy attitude on Melanie's part, April didn't go home until she felt sure they had reached a firm decision. No matter what, no new girl was going to be let in on the Egypt Game. If they asked Elizabeth to walk to school with them, and maybe talked to her at recesses for a while, until she got around to making fourth-grade friends, that would be enough.

The next morning April and Melanie went dutifully down the little dark basement hallway and knocked on the door of the Chungs' apartment. Almost immediately the door across the hall opened and Mr. Bodler, the janitor, looked out. "Oh, hello there, young ladies," he said. "Thought I heard someone knocking on my door."

"Hello, Mr. Bodler," Melanie said. "We've come

to get the new girl and take her to school with us."

"Well now, isn't that nice. I think that's right nice of you young ladies."

April and Melanie turned back to the Chungs' door, but Mr. Bodler went on standing behind them. They exchanged sideways "wouldn't you know it" glances. Mr. Bodler was a fattish man with faded blond hair who was always nosily cheerful at children. The situation was already uncomfortable, and Mr. Bodler, who was a naturally uncomfortable person to be around, wasn't making it any better.

The door of the Chungs' apartment was finally opened by a very small Asian girl. "Hi," April said. "Is your big sister ready for school? We've come to take her."

The girl smiled shyly. "I'm Elizabeth," she said.

On the way to school Elizabeth walked between April and Melanie. She really was amazingly tiny for a fourth grader. Her thick black hair was pulled back into a carefully curled ponytail that bounced when she walked. And there was something about the carved perfection of her face that made her smile seem like magic—an enchanted ivory princess warming suddenly to life. She was shy, but not in the stiff embarrassing way that makes other people feel embarrassed, too. It was a gentle friendly shyness that made other people feel important, sort of in charge of things.

April had been afraid—well, looking at Elizabeth's upturned face and pretty tilted eyes, wide with wonder at almost anything you told her, it was hard to remember just what she had been afraid of. She almost wished she hadn't been so convincing when she talked to Melanie the night before about how they didn't want anbody else butting into their friendship.

By the time April and Melanie delivered Elizabeth to the door of the fourth-grade room, they had completely forgotten that taking care of Elizabeth had been anybody's idea but their own. Melanie's forehead wrinkled with worry as she watched Elizabeth make her way timidly through the noisily assembling fourth graders, to the teacher's desk. And a couple of boys who were saying, "Hey, look at the new girl!" and, "Ugh! A girl!" and other typically fourth-grade remarks were suddenly silenced when they met April's ferocious glare.

That afternoon April and Melanie walked Elizabeth home and by the next morning they were both wondering if it wouldn't be all right, after all, to let her join the Egypt Game. But it was a touchy sort of thing to bring up, not knowing for sure how the other one felt about it. And then a very strange thing happened.

Elizabeth had arranged to meet them that morning on the front steps of the Casa Rosada and when April and Melanie were crossing the lobby they could see her through the glass of the front door. She was sitting on the railing and looking off up Orchard Avenue so her profile was towards them. All of a sudden April grabbed Melanie's arm. "Look!" she whispered.

"What?" Melanie whispered back.

"Elizabeth," April said. "Who does she look like?"

Melanie caught her breath. "Nefertiti," she breathed.

Sure enough. Elizabeth's ponytail pulled her hair

back away from her face and neck; and there was certainly something about her delicate, slender-necked profile that was very like the statue of Nefertiti. Of course, Elizabeth's nose was a tiny bit shorter and maybe her chin a little rounder, but the resemblance was there just the same.

She saw them then and bounced through the door to meet them before anything more could be said, but it wasn't really necessary. April and Melanie just looked at each other and nodded, and on the way to school they started telling Elizabeth all about the Egypt Game.

Prisoners of Fear

ELIZABETH TURNED OUT TO BE JUST WHAT THE Egypt Game needed to make it perfect. Of course, she didn't have many ideas; but then, she was younger and hadn't had a chance to learn much about ancient history. Besides, April and Melanie had almost more ideas than they could use anyway. Elizabeth helped in other ways.

She was just crazy about every part of the Egypt Game, and she was full of admiring comments. For instance, she loved the "Hymn to Isis" that Melanie had made up almost by herself, with just a little bit of help from a book of Egyptian poetry. Elizabeth said it was the most beautiful thing she'd ever heard. And the first time she saw April do a ceremony for Set she kept jumping up and down with half-scared excitement. For a few days it was fun just doing everything over for Elizabeth to appreciate; and after that they got around to starting a new part of the game. In the new part, Marshall finally got to be the young pharaoh, Marshamosis, again, and Elizabeth was the queen, Neferbeth. April and Melanie were priestesses. First they were evil priestesses, leading Marshamosis and Neferbeth into the clutches of the wicked Set. And then they were priestesses of Isis coming to the rescue.

That was about where they were in the Game, when something happened that almost put an end to the Egypt Game; and not to the Egypt Game alone, but to all the outdoor games in the whole neighborhood. On that particular afternoon, the girls had built a dungeon out of cardboard boxes in the corner of the storage yard. Elizabeth and Marshall were languishing in the dungeon, tied hand and foot, victims of the priests of Set. April and Melanie were creeping cautiously from pillar to pillar in the Temple of Evil, on their way to the rescue. Melanie was crouching behind an imaginary pillar, when suddenly she straightened up and stood listening. In the dungeon Elizabeth heard it too, and quickly untied her bonds. April ran to help Marshall with his. They were really only kite string and knotted easily. From somewhere not too far away, perhaps the main alley behind the Casa Rosada, Mrs. Ross's voice was calling, "Melanie! Marshall! Melanie!" There was something about the tone of her voice that made Melanie's eyes widen with fear.

"Something's wrong," she said.

"It's too early." April nodded. "She never gets home this early."

They scrambled through the hole in the fence and, dragging Marshall to hurry him up, they dashed for the main alley behind the Casa Rosada. From there they could safely answer without giving the location of Egypt away.

Mrs. Ross met them near the back door of the apartment house. Even though they all clamored to know what was the matter, she only shook her head and said, "There's been some trouble in the neighborhood. April, you and Elizabeth come up to our apartment until your folks get home."

Of course they were all terribly curious, but Mrs. Ross wouldn't say any more. "We'll wait to discuss it until we have the facts," she said. "What I know right now amounts only to rumors. There may not be any truth in the story at all."

It occurred to all of them, though, that the rumors had been frightening enough to make Mrs. Ross cancel her after-school remedial reading class—which she almost never did—and come home early. And Melanie noticed a strangeness in her voice and that her hand shook as she put milk and cookies on the table. It had to be something serious.

By the next day it was common knowledge. A little girl who lived in the neighborhood had been killed. She hadn't gone to Wilson School, so April and Melanie had barely known her, but her home was only a few blocks away from the Casa Rosada. Like all children in the neighborhood, and in all neighborhoods for that matter, she had been warned about strangers —but she must have forgotten. She had been on her way to the drugstore—the very one where April had purchased her eyelashes—in the early evening, and she had never returned. The next day her body had been found in the marshland near the bay.

It was a terrible and shocking thing. But there was something else, another circumstance, that made it even more terrifying and threatening to the parents of the neighborhood. It had happened before. Almost a year before, a little boy from the same area had disappeared in almost the same way; and the police were saying that it looked as if the guilty person was a resident of the neighborhood.

As the days passed and no arrests were made, fear and suspicion grew and spread in all directions; and a great silence began to settle over Orchard Avenue and the streets and alleys on either side.

Twice a day a few children could be seen walking to and from school, but they went quickly and in larger groups than usual; and many other parents arranged car pools, even for children who had only a few blocks to walk. Afternoons and weekends, which usually rang with a medley of shouts and laughter and pounding feet, dragged by in a strange, uneasy silence broken only by the dull hum of traffic.

But although fear made a great silence out-of-doors, inside the homes and stores and apartments it had a different sound—it talked and it talked and it talked. For the boys and girls, talking was about all there was left to do, since nobody was being allowed to play outside. Lying across a bed, or sitting on one of the Casa Rosada's little iron balconies, April and Melanie talked it over many times. Most of their special information, besides what they read in the papers, came from Mrs. Ross by way of Melanie. Caroline didn't seem to know how to talk about important or shocking things, and April wouldn't have asked her.

"I wonder why anyone would do an awful thing like that?" April asked one day while she and Melanie were sitting on the floor in Melanie's bedroom, looking through old magazines for new people for the paper-families game. "On TV and in the movies when somebody gets killed it's usually because of money, or else revenge. But little kids don't have that much money and there's all sorts of ways to get revenge on kids without doing a thing like that."

Melanie looked at April curiously. She'd noticed before that April, in spite of her sophisticated ways, really didn't know much at all about certain kinds of

71

things. The kinds of things parents tell their children when they're alone together and other kids tell you if they know you really well. All April's information seemed to be the kind of things grown-ups let you overhear, and of course, nearly everything she could find in the children's part of libraries.

"They do it because they're sick," Melanie answered. "That's what my mom says. It's a sickness of the mind. They can't help themselves, so there's no use hating them, but they just have to be caught and shut up or they'll probably do it again."

"But why can't they catch him, if he's crazy? It seems to me a crazy person wouldn't be hard to catch."

"It's not like that," Melanie said. "My mom says some people who are crazy are only crazy at times, or in certain ways. Most of the time they seem just like anybody. My mom says that's why kids have to be careful about all strangers, no matter if they seem as nice as anything."

"Yeah," April said. "I guess that's right. You can usually tell about people if you watch them hard, but I guess you can't always. Hey, look. Here's a mother who's just right for the haunted house family. Isn't she weird?"

It wasn't only the boys and girls of Orchard Avenue who talked and talked. The grown-ups did, too. Everybody had theories and opinions, and everybody had heard rumors they were eager to repeat. There was one rumor that was particularly persistent and particularly troublesome to the members of the Egypt Game. It had to do with the Professor.

Someone had seen two policemen going into the Professor's store on the morning after the little girl had disappeared. It looked as if he must be a suspect, at least. No one knew that the Professor was guilty; but at the same time, no one knew anything about him that would make them believe he was innocent. There were other people in the neighborhood who were noted for their bad tempers or downright meanness, but their actions were predictable. For instance, you knew that Mrs. Harkness would call the police if you stepped on her lawn, and that at Schmitt's Variety Store you'd get cheated out of small change if you weren't careful. But how could anyone know what a person like the Professor would do? Of course, he hadn't been arrested yet, but that might only mean that the police hadn't found the proof.

Only the Egypt gang maintained that the Professor was innocent. April said she was sure of it because of a feeling she had. As just about the only kid in the neighborhood who'd actually talked to the Professor, she felt she was entitled to have feelings about what he might do. Melanie and Elizabeth thought the Professor was innocent because April did. And, without really admitting it even to themselves, all three of them kept thinking he must be innocent because if he was guilty the Egypt Game was ruined forever. Nobody plays games in the backyard of a murderer.

But apparently there were other people who were just as firmly convinced of the old man's guilt. Three days after the murder someone threw a brick through one of his store's show windows, and Mr. Schmitt organized a not-so-secret campaign to get people to write letters and sign petitions inviting the Professor to leave the neighborhood. The fact that the Professor sold old and cheap some of the things that Mr. Schmitt sold new and expensive was worth thinking about; but it really didn't prove anything one way or the other.

Without the Egypt Game the days were very slow for the four Egyptians. Once or twice they tried to play the Game indoors, before the grown-ups were at home of course; but it wasn't the same at all. In fact, it was such a disappointment that it was frightening. What if the magic was gone forever? But probably it was only that carpets and couches and curtains just didn't make the right atmosphere for a game about hidden splendors and giant mysteries, in a land of mud and sand. Anyway, they decided instead to spend their time making some things they could use when they finally could return to Egypt.

Elizabeth, who was very clever and artistic with

her hands, started the costume idea by making herself a Nefertiti headdress out of a plastic bleach bottle with the top cut off. Next, Melanie got some old curtains from her mother, enough to make sheer flowing robes for everyone. The sheer robes were to be worn over short tunics made of pillowcases.

It was April who got the idea of going around the apartment house and asking all the ladies if they had any old junk jewelry that they were willing to sell. Just as she predicted, most people gave them stuff and refused to take any money, which was just as well, since they only had nineteen cents between them. Some of the jewelry they took apart and glued or sewed onto their robes for decoration; but some of the necklaces and bracelets that looked a little bit Egyptian they used just as they were.

Their most successful creation was Marshall's costume. One day when they were all working in the Rosses' apartment, Marshall got out his indoor bowling game. The ball and tenpins were made of a light plastic, so as not to dent up the furniture. April was watching him set up the pins and suddenly got a brilliant idea. She went upstairs, got one of her Egypt books, and showed the rest of them that the tenpins were shaped exactly like the inner part of the double crown of Egypt. The outer part could be made of another bleach bottle. Melanie wasn't sure they ought to use up one of Marshall's tenpins; but April pointed out that there was nothing wrong with the game of ninepins. And, anyway, they were Marshall's and he was all for it when he found out the crown was to be for him. When it was all put together and painted, with a cardboard vulture's head and cobra glued to the front, it looked so impressive they could hardly believe they'd made it themselves.

With no place to work but their own rooms, it wasn't long, of course, until their families knew the girls were making Egyptian costumes. But fortunately

a simple and logical explanation was handy. Halloween wasn't far away and making costumes was a perfectly natural thing to be doing.

As the days went by, the headlines about the terrible thing that had happened near Orchard Avenue got smaller and smaller. The paper said the police were "following up leads" and "investigating clues," but no arrests were made and gradually people stopped talking about it so much. The Professor still stubbornly opened his store every day, but now he had almost no local trade. The few people who had gone in now and then to look over his used merchandise department were staying away, and only an occasional out-of-town antique buyer was seen entering his store. People wondered how he managed to stay in business, and they wondered if he was really guilty, and they wondered . . . But wondering takes time, and most of the people of the neighborhood were hard-working people, and so they gradually began to forget. And very gradually the children began to play out-of-doors again. But the Rosses and Mrs. Chung were frustratingly careful parents, and it looked as if they were going to be the very last ones to stop worrying. Of course, Caroline Hall hadn't given April permission to play outside either; but she didn't get home until 5:30, and April just might have been willing to do a little private forgetting on her own if she'd had anyone to keep her company. But since Elizabeth and Melanie were stuck inside, April figured she might as well be, too.

The waiting was particularly hard on April because, without the Egypt Game to think about, it was more difficult to keep from thinking about other things. At first it was the empty mailbox to try not to think about—not a single letter from Dorothea for over a month. And then at last there was a letter—and even more to worry about. Dorothea was back in Hollywood. She must have gotten all of April's letters, but she didn't even mention the question that April asked in every one. Dorothea wrote about her tour, and about her new job in a nightclub, and about Nick; but she said nothing at all about April's coming home.

As the days dragged by, the Egypt gang grew more and more impatient. They knew that Egypt was waiting for them just as they had left it because several times they had been able to stop by on their way to school. They had had time to notice things— important things—like the fact that the Crocodile Stone seemed to have moved a tiny bit, a sure sign of its sinister power, and that the flowers on the altar of Nefertiti stayed fresh much longer than you'd expect, as if in tribute to her beauty. But there was no time for a real game because Mrs. Ross had arranged for a neighbor lady who didn't work to make sure they arrived home safely and on time.

So the days passed and the Egyptian clothing grew fancier and all sorts of new plans were made for the time when they could return to Egypt.

Summoned by the Mighty Ones

RIGHT UP UNTIL A FEW DAYS BEFORE THE END OF the month it really looked as if Halloween was going to be completely wasted. Of course, there was going to be a program at school and kids who wanted to could wear their costumes to afternoon classes, but only little primary kids got very excited about that. The real fun of Halloween, trick-or-treating and being allowed to tear around out-of-doors late at night, was absolutely out. At least that was what all the parents in the neighborhood were saying all month long. Unless, of course, the murderer had been caught by then. But as day after day went by with nothing new in the papers, there seemed little hope of that. And then, with only three more days to go, suddenly there was good news.

At a P.T.A. meeting at Wilson School, a couple of

really red-blooded mothers stood up and volunteered their husbands to take large groups of trick-or-treaters around the neighborhood. Before long some other fathers got shamed or nagged into doing the same thing, and by the day before Halloween nearly all the kids at Wilson were signed up to go around trick-or-treating with some large, chaperoned group.

Mr. Barkley and Mr. Kamata were going to be the chaperones for all the kids who lived in the Casa Rosada and the rest of the eight hundred block of Orchard Avenue. Mr. Barkley was the father of some six-year-old twins who lived on the first floor of the Casa Rosada, and Mr. Kamata was from Kamata's Realty, just across the street, and the father of Ken Kamata, who was in April and Melanie's class at Wilson. April had it figured out that there were at least twenty-five kids who would be going with Mr. Barkley and Mr. Kamata, and that was a lot of kids to keep track of, particularly in the dark. Which opened the way for a fascinating and frightening scheme.

If, April decided, the Egypt gang all stayed together, there might be a chance to slip away from the big group to pay a visit to Egypt. Their flashlights and jack-o'-lanterns would be enough to light up the storage yard at least a little, and it would be really terrific—a nighttime ceremony in the spooky half-light, and with everybody wearing their new

Egyptian costumes. They would only stay for a few minutes, and they'd get back to the trick-or-treaters before they were missed.

When April first told Melanie about her plan, Melanie thought it was just about the most exciting idea she'd ever heard. She agreed to everything, even to not telling Elizabeth until Halloween night so that she wouldn't have too long to worry about it. Elizabeth had a tendency to worry about things like not having permission. She might not understand that it was not at all like being downright disobedient. As April pointed out, no one had forbidden them to visit Egypt on Halloween night. Melanie did just mention that maybe that was because nobody knew about Egypt; but April just grinned and said, "Yeah, I know. Lucky, isn't it."

Later, when Melanie began to think about it in private, she began to have some doubts. Even though the Egypt gang had decided that the Professor was innocent, what if they just might be wrong? Or what if the Professor was innocent, but the somebody else who wasn't really did live right in the neighborhood, as so many people seemed to think? In that case a trip to Egypt might be a lot worse than downright disobedient. It might be deadly dangerous. *Downright disobedient* and *deadly dangerous*. The two phrases seemed to get stuck in Melanie's head. The night before Halloween she woke up several times with those four words throbbing through her thoughts. By morning she'd decided to tell April that she'd changed her mind.

But the next day Melanie had an early-morning piano lesson, so there was no time to talk to April before school. And at school there were always too many people around. Even though Melanie tried all day to find an opportunity, she still hadn't told April about her decision when the time came to get into their costumes.

April had been keeping all the costumes in a box in her closet, and it had been decided that they would all get ready at her place. On the way up Melanie and Marshall met Elizabeth in the hall. Melanie had been almost hoping that Elizabeth would have her two sisters along. That would have put an end to the Egypt question without her having to say anything. But no such luck. Elizabeth explained that her little sisters were staying home because they were afraid of the dark and of all the big kids in their costumes.

When they reached April's apartment, Mrs. Hall met them at the door. "Come in, come in," she said. "April's all dressed already. She's in her room."

April looked great. She was wearing her Egyptian headdress and under her sheer jeweled robe she had on the short tunic made of a pillowcase. Around the bottom of the pillowcase there were Egyptian-looking decorations done in red and black crayon. But best of all were her face and hair. For once her false eyelashes were on straight, and she had heavy black eye makeup that made her eyes look long and mysterious. But most surprising was her hair—it was cut short in a sort of Cleopatra bob.

"Caroline helped me with my face and hair," April said, and she looked at Caroline and smiled. It occurred to Melanie that it was the first time she'd ever seen April smile at her grandmother. It also occurred to her that April wasn't going to be able to wear an upsweep anymore, but she didn't say anything about that.

Instead. she only said, "Your hair looks terrific, April. You ought to wear it that way all the time."

Mrs. Hall reminded them that they better hurry so they wouldn't keep the other trick-or-treaters waiting and then she went out and left them alone. April shut the door of her room behind her grandmother and then she turned around very slowly and dramatically to face the rest of the Egypt gang. One look at her face and Melanie had a strong feeling that *downright disobedient* and even *deadly dangerous* weren't going to be enough. She felt herself slipping before she was even sure of the direction in which they were moving.

April put her arms down stiffly along her sides and with her eyes closed she tilted her Egyptian face upward raptly. To Melanie she looked like a miniature monolith, glowing with mystery. "We have received a message," April whispered with her eyes still closed. "We are summoned by the mighty ones, the mighty ones of Egypt."

"The mighty ones?" Elizabeth's voice quavered a little.

April snapped back into life and snatched up something from her dresser. It was a little velvet pin-cushion box that she kept special things on. "It's in here," she said, holding the box out dramatically until they had all gathered around.

"The summons from Set and Isis," Melanie said. It was a statement instead of a question; and with a last lingering dismay she realized that she was already using her high priestess voice. April nodded and her eyes flicked across Melanie's in the way they always did when their imaginations were tuned in. The gods of Egypt struggled with the gods of conscience, and Egypt won. "The mighty ones have summoned us," Melanie chanted and dropped to her knees.

Following Melanie's lead, April was on her knees almost as quickly and Elizabeth and Marshall weren't far behind. Slowly and with drama April opened the box. There, on a cushion of paper handkerchiefs, was a single shiny feather. "Just a few minutes ago," April whispered, "I heard something—a strange sound —outside my window. I'd been expecting something.

I'd had a weird feeling all day long. Hadn't you?"
They all nodded and Melanie didn't even remember
what kind of feelings she'd really been having all day.
"So I ran to the window and threw it open and there
it was—right on the sill. A token—from the mighty
ones."

"Evil Set and Beautiful Isis have sent us a token,"
Melanie chanted. She nudged Elizabeth with her elbow and whispered, "You say, 'The mighty ones have
summoned us to their temple.'"

"The mighty ones have summoned us to their temple." Elizabeth imitated Melanie's singing chant.

April poked Marshall. "You say, 'We have received
your summons, O mighty ones.'"

"We have received your summons, O mighty
ones," Marshall chanted and then ad-libbed, "and
it's nothing but an old pigeon feather." He scanned
the girls' faces expectantly, but they chose to ignore
him.

While they were getting into their costumes, Elizabeth asked a few worried questions about what they
were going to do, but April only said, "I don't know.
We'll have to stick close together and look for a sign."

"What sort of a sign?" Elizabeth wanted to know.

"A secret omen," Melanie said.

"Will it be a pigeon feather?" Marshall asked.

"We don't know what it will be," April told him.

"But we will know it when it appears." She clasped her hands and struck a wonder-and-amazement pose. "The very air will smell of mystery," she breathed.

Marshall sniffed thoughtfully as April got him into his crown and robe and tried to make his baby-round eyes look long and mysterious with the eyebrow pencil. She was more successful with Elizabeth's and Melanie's eyes. They both had beautiful eyes anyway—Elizabeth's were exotic, long and tilted, and Melanie's were luxurious, velvet and ivory, fringed with black silk. With the Egyptian makeup they both looked fantastic.

By the time they had gotten Elizabeth's ponytail tucked inside her Nefertiti headdress it was almost 7:00. They started to rush out, but in the hallway they noticed that Marshall wasn't with them. They dashed back and found him in the closet with April's pin-box. He was calm as they grabbed him out of the closet, snatched away the pin-box and scolded him across the living room to the hall door. "I was just smelling the mystery, like April said," he was explaining patiently, when suddenly he grabbed hold of the door frame and howled, "STOP!" The result was a four-way collision of Egyptians in the doorway. Marshall kept on yelling, "Stop!" and Elizabeth yelled "Ouch!" because somebody stepped on her, and April yelled, "What the ——!"

But Melanie knew right away what the matter was. She ran back into the bedroom and got Security from where he'd been left on April's bed, and at last the Egyptians were on their way.

The Return to Egypt

THE TRICK-OR-TREAT GROUP WAS A MILLING MOB of devils, witches, tramps and monsters. Mr. Barkley, who always acted as if being the father of six-year-old twin boys was almost more than he could stand, looked positively exhausted; and even Mr. Kamata's sturdy real-estate-salesman's smile was beginning to wilt. Outside the Casa Rosada a black cat, a mechanical man, a Little Red Riding Hood, two tramps and four ancient Egyptians joined the already unwieldy group.

They had started off up Orchard Avenue in a sprawly column when Marshall suddenly stopped and tugged at Melanie's arm. "I want a sign," he said loudly. Several of the surrounding trick-or-treaters turned to look at him, and the other three Egyptians stared in astonishment. Marshall had never blabbed about secrets before.

"Shhh!" April hissed. "Not yet! I'll tell you when."

"Shhh, Marshall. It's a secret," Elizabeth whispered covering his mouth with her hand.

"What's the matter with you?" Melanie asked in astonishment.

Marshall pushed Elizabeth's hand away. "Not a secret sign," he said. "A sign to carry."

All of a sudden Melanie laughed. "Oh," she said, "I guess he thinks we're a demonstration—like at the university. He's never been trick-or-treating because he was too young last year. But he knows about demonstrations."

Everybody laughed, except Marshall. "We're not a demonstration, Marshall," Melanie explained, tugging at him to get him moving again. "We're trick-or-treating. Trick-or-treating is for candy and demonstrations are for things like Peace and Freedom. It's different."

Marshall relaxed and allowed himself to be pulled down the street, but he didn't look convinced. "*I'm* a demonstration," he said firmly.

When the crowd turned up Elm Street where there were more good houses to visit, the Egyptians began to drop to the rear of the group where it would

be easier to get away. That meant they were the last ones up to each home, and sometimes most of the good stuff was already taken; but they hardly noticed. They were too busy looking for an omen.

At the last house before they turned off Elm Street, the Egypt gang started up the front walk and collided with two other trick-or-treaters who also seemed to be hanging behind the main group—a monster and a walking pile of boxes. "Hey," the monster said, "it's Ross and February. What are you supposed to be?"

The rubber monster mask completely covered the speaker's head, but the voice was familiar; and besides, the sixth-grade boys were the only ones who called April, February. Then the walking boxes said, "Hey man! It's a whole herd of Egyptians." He poked Marshall in the stomach and said, "Hi there, King Tut."

"Okay, Mr. Wise-Guy Alvillar," Melanie said. "I know who you are." She turned to April with an exasperated shrug. "It's Kamata and Alvillar."

Ken Kamata and Toby Alvillar were just about the most disgusting boys in the sixth grade, in a fascinating sort of way. They were best friends and always together, and everybody always voted for them for everything and wanted to be on their team. But not April and Melanie. April and Melanie always told each other that Ken and Toby were just ordinary (ugh) boys, and it was stupid the way everybody treated them so special. April and Melanie just couldn't figure out what people saw in them.

Of course, Toby had a special talent for getting people off the hook by making the teacher laugh. Just when Mrs. Granger was really building up a head of steam over something, Toby would make some little remark and Mrs. Granger would start choking and have to turn her back. Sometimes she'd try to pick things up where she left off, but all that lost momentum made a big difference.

Ken *was* sort of cute in a big blunt cocky way. He had a clean-cut all-American-Asian look about him, and he walked with a high-school swagger. Toby was thinner, with big ears that stuck out of his shaggy hair and enormous brown eyes that were always up to something, like a pair of TV screens turned on full blast. But right now you couldn't see what either one of them really looked like at all.

Ken had a man's old overcoat on over a pillow-padded hunchback, and (wouldn't you know it) rubber monster hands and feet, too, as well as the mask. Ken's father sold a lot of real estate and he could afford expensive stuff like that. Toby was the box man. He had a small box over his head, with a Saran Wrap–covered opening shaped like a TV screen to look out through. The rest of him was covered with all sorts of other boxes all strung together and painted black and covered with pasted-on ads out of papers and magazines. There were Alka-Seltzer and Pepto-Bismol ads pasted on his stomach box, aspirin ads on his head box, and even a deodorant ad under his left arm.

"Boy! Are you two in character," April said. "A monster and a pile of junk."

"I'll have you know that I represent the New American," Toby said haughtily. Then he grinned. "It was my dad's idea. He says it's a new art form he just invented."

Toby's dad had been a graduate student at the university. He was also a sculptor who made statues out of all kinds of junk.

"An art form!" April said. "Well, all I can say is—"

"Don't," Toby interrupted. "You'd just show off your ignorance."

"Come on, Tobe," Ken said. "We're getting left behind."

"Yeah, you little kids ought to keep up with the group better," Toby said, as he started off up the sidewalk. "You're liable to get hurt."

"Little kids!" Melanie yelled after him. "Look who's talking!"

Marshall ran after Toby and gave him a shove on the rear of his biggest box. "We're not little kids," he said, "We're Egyptians."

Toby swiveled his TV head around and surveyed the damage. "Hey, watch it!" he said. "You just bent my Jockey shorts ad."

April and Melanie didn't believe in encouraging Toby by laughing at him, but that was too much. By the time the Egyptians got over their convulsions of giggles, Ken and Toby had disappeared around the corner, and the lady whose walk they were on was calling to ask if they wanted some candy or not.

After that Melanie suggested that maybe they'd better stay up with the group a little better or the fathers would notice and start watching them. But even when they were trying, it wasn't easy to catch up because their costumes were such a success. At almost every house they had to be admired and questioned and other members of the family had to be called to see them—particularly Elizabeth and Marshall. Everyone thought Elizabeth and Marshall were just "darling," and "adorable," and they had to be admired and fussed over before the Egyptians could take their candy and leave.

At last, at one house they had to wait while the man got his flash camera out to take their picture, and when they finally got away and rushed down the stairs the big group of trick-or-treaters had completely disappeared.

There they were, all alone on the dimly lit sidewalk, and it was suddenly very quiet. They ran down the block to the corner, where they could look all four ways, but still there wasn't a person in sight. They were still just standing there looking around and wondering what to do, when suddenly Melanie pointed at the horizon. "Look," she said. "A shooting star!"

"A shooting star!" Everybody repeated it in whispered unison as if they'd been rehearsed. Then everybody looked at April. She nodded. "The secret omen," she said slowly, making every syllable heavy with significance. Marshall started turning around and around, smelling the air.

Looking around one last time to be sure no one was watching, the girls grabbed Marshall out of his tailspin and started down the sidewalk in the direction that they had come. They scurried down two blocks without seeing a soul, turned the corner, and a moment later ducked into the alley that led to Egypt.

If the secret and mysterious land of Egypt was fascinating in the daytime, it was doubly so at night. Dimly lit by a distant streetlight, two flashlights, and a jack-o'-lantern, it was almost too fascinating to bear. April told everyone to wait just inside the fence while she tiptoed forward and lit the cone of incense on the altar of Set and the two candles that stood before the goddess Isis. Then she motioned everyone forward.

"The Great Ceremony of the Celebration of the Return to Egypt has begun!" she chanted, and all four Egyptians prostrated themselves before the egg crate and the birdbath.

Egypt Invaded

APRIL AND MELANIE ROSE TO THEIR KNEES FROM their deep bows before the double altars of Egypt. Over the heads of Elizabeth and Marshall they exchanged a glance that said, "Okay. What's next?" Melanie reached over absently to help Marshall with his pharaoh's crown, which had slipped down over his eyes while he was touching his forehead to the floor. Suddenly her eyes lit up with an "I have it" expression. She gave the crown a final tug down over Marshall's ears and turned to face the altar of Set. She raised her arms and April quickly followed suit.

"The gods are angry at us for being gone so long," she chanted.

"The gods are angry," April repeated. A quick glare at Elizabeth and Marshall got them going.

"The gods are angry," they parroted.

Melanie nodded and continued with her inspiration. "The gods demand that we make a sacrifice so that we may be forgiven." She looked over at April, and April nodded delightedly.

"The gods demand that we make a horrible and bloody sacrifice." April took up Melanie's theme with relish.

"A horrible and bloody sacrifice," Melanie agreed.

"A horrible and bloody sacrifice," Marshall and Elizabeth repeated dutifully, but Elizabeth's voice quavered a little and Marshall leaned over and poked his sister.

"What sort of bloody?" he demanded in a whisper.

But now April was off and away, and Melanie was following. "The gods will tell us what the sacrifice must be," April said. "We must approach the altar one at a time and touch the Crocodile Stone, the sacred symbol of Set. We must touch the sacred symbol of Set and wait for a message about the sacrifice. Then we will decide whose message is the best."

April went first. She approached the egg crate using the correct Egyptian walk, which was done by walking with your shoulders sideways, arms held out from the body and bent sharply at the wrist. In front of the altar she bowed deeply with her head tucked between her upraised arms, and then placed her fingertips on the Crocodile Stone. She stood for a minute with her face turned upward. Melanie poked the other kids and motioned for them to watch closely.

When April stalked back to them looking wildly secretive, Melanie walked up to the altar and followed her example, doing exactly the same things. Then came Elizabeth's turn and finally Marshall's. Then they all sat down in a circle on the floor.

As soon as everyone was seated, Elizabeth raised her hand and shook it frantically. She was looking excited and pleasantly surprised with herself. She had just had a terribly daring idea and she couldn't wait to tell it.

"All right, Elizabeth first," Melanie said. "Okay, April?"

April nodded. "Go ahead, Neferbeth," she said, "but put your hand down, for heaven's sake. You're not in school, you're a lady pharaoh."

Elizabeth snatched her hand down and suggested eagerly that Set's message was that they should stick their fingers with a needle and write him a letter in their own blood.

April and Melanie exchanged surprised and appreciative glances, and Elizabeth beamed proudly. She didn't think it was necessary to mention that her teacher had just read *Tom Sawyer* to the class—and just possibly Set had had a little help from Mark Twain.

However, there was one small detail—nobody had a needle. Elizabeth looked crushed. "Don't feel bad,

Bethy," Melanie said. "It was a neat idea."

"I'll say," April agreed. "It was a terrific idea."

"It was a dumb idea," Marshall muttered. "When you stick your finger you get infested."

"Infected," Melanie corrected. "You go next, April."

April made a trance-like face. "When I stood before the altar," she chanted, "I heard the voice of the Crocodile god. He said the object to be sacrificed must be something very dear to us. It must be something we hate to part with. Otherwise it won't count. The Crocodile god has told me that we must sacrifice"—she pointed dramatically—"Security!"

"NO!" Marshall shouted, jumping up and hugging Security to his chest. "NO! NO! NO!" With every shout he stamped his foot. All three girls were around him in a moment, shushing and begging him to keep still. He shushed, but he went over to the edge of the shed and stood with his back to them.

"All right, Marshall. We won't sacrifice Security. Will we, April?" Melanie said.

April went into a quick trance with her fingers to her forehead. "The gods have changed their minds," she announced in a moment. "They say they don't want Security. But just don't *yell* like that anymore. Somebody will hear us, and we'll get caught."

"Somebody already heard us," Marshall muttered darkly.

"What do you mean, somebody already heard us?" Melanie gasped. But Marshall only shrugged and said nothing more.

"Come on back to the circle," Melanie coaxed. "We take it all back about Security. Besides, it's your turn to say what the message was."

Marshall allowed himself to be led back to the circle, but his chin was still sticking out, and he was glaring at April. He put his hand to his forehead the way April had done and then jerked it away. "Let's sacrifice April," he suggested.

That gave everybody the giggles, and finally Marshall broke down and smiled, too. Then it was Melanie's turn. Melanie said that she had read about some people who cut off their fingers as sacrifices. At that point even April looked shocked, and Elizabeth almost fainted. But Melanie only laughed. "I didn't mean we should do *that*," she said. "It just gave me an idea. We could pull out some hairs—and maybe cut off some fingernails."

"No scissors," Elizabeth reminded with just a touch of satisfaction.

"We could bite them off," April suggested. "I do it all the time."

A few minutes later a small fire of twisted paper was burning in the mixing bowl fire-pit, and the high priestesses (and junior high priest) of Egypt were parading in a circle before the altar. They were walking in the Egyptian manner—one shoulder forward, arms bent at the wrist—except from time to time when they had to chew off another fingernail. Now and then one or another would approach the altar, bow and drop a scrap of humanity on the flames: a hair or two or a shred of fingernail.

It was just about the best ceremony they'd ever had, and it was a shame to end it; but Melanie was just thinking that perhaps it was time to leave when suddenly she heard Elizabeth give a gasp of pure terror. Following Elizabeth's gaze, Melanie was horrified to see a huge misshapen figure teetering on the top of the high board fence. The figure teetered wildly in the dim light, and then sprang forward to land in a horrible threatening crouch, right in the middle of Egypt.

Elizabethan Diplomacy

WHEN THE SHAPELESS INHUMAN FIGURE SPRANG INTO the middle of the storage yard, the four Egyptians could only clutch each other in panic, too shocked for the moment to even scream. April had just managed to get her mouth open to yell for help, when suddenly Marshall pointed and said, "Look." A second figure was appearing over the top of the fence.

This second invader, who was having some difficulty climbing over the wire at the top of the fence, had a strangely angular look about him. Strangely angular—and strangely familiar. In all four Egyptians frozen fear boiled at once into a choking mixture of anger and relief. In April it overflowed in stuttering sputter. "You—you d-d-dirty f-f-finks!" she yelled.

On top of the fence Toby finally managed to get his boxy legs free of the barbed wire. He jumped down, losing his TV head in the process. Then, as the four badly shaken Egyptians turned loose of each other and tried to regain their dignity, the monster and the box-man leaned on each other and choked with fiendish laughter.

They laughed leaning on each other and standing up—bending over as if they were in pain—and finally collapsed, sitting flat on the ground. Then, while the four members of the Egypt gang stared at them in helpless fuming anger, they just sat there, leaning against each other's backs, still shaking with gradually weakening seizures.

"Man—oh—man!" Toby gasped finally. "I've got to quit laughing. My stomach's killing me."

"Sheesh! Me too," Ken said. "I'm dying." Ken fell over backwards and just lay there, holding his stomach and saying "Sheesh" weakly from time to time. But Toby crossed his legs and leaned forward with his chin on one hand and stared at the angry Egyptians.

"Hey, February," he said finally. "How do you say panic button in Egyptian?"

April clenched her fists and took a step forward. Toby started to scramble to his feet—he'd seen April in action before. But Melanie and Elizabeth grabbed her and held her back.

"Turn loose," April said. "I'm going to punch him in the nose."

"There's no use doing that," Melanie whispered. "That won't do any good. We can't keep them from telling on us by punching them in the nose."

After a moment's consideration April nodded. ".Okay. Turn loose. I won't punch them. At least not till we find out what they're going to do." She unclenched her fists and all three girls approached the enemy. Left behind, Marshall sat down on the edge of the temple floor in a good position to watch everything that might happen. Both the boys were standing now, watching the girls warily.

"Well," Melanie began. "Are you going to tell on us, or not?"

"Tell on you?" Ken said. "What makes you think we'd do a thing like that?"

"Of course not," Toby said. "We don't go around finking on people." The girls glanced at each other in surprised relief. "However," Toby continued, "this is not a matter of plain and simple finking. Letting you Egyptians get away with all this secret stuff just might be considered—like, unpatriotic, or something."

"Hey, you're right," Ken said. "Maybe we ought to tell the F.B.I."

"Maybe we should. Or maybe we could just make an official report on the whole scene—like, for current events tomorrow morning." Toby stalked to the middle of the yard in what was obviously meant to be the Egyptian walk. Then he faced the group, cleared his throat, and in a phony voice he said, " 'What's Happening in Egypt'—a very official report by Tobias Alvillar, Secret Agent."

Toby was pretty funny all right, but no one laughed but Ken. April was thinking a horrible thought. If they knew about the Egyptian walk, how much else did they know? Up until then she'd been thinking that the fence was too high to look over—and they couldn't have seen very much while they were scrambling over it. She ran to the loose board and looked out into the alley. When she pulled her head back in, Melanie guessed the awful truth before she heard it.

Taking Melanie aside, April whispered, "There are boxes piled up out there. They could have been watching forever! Shall I punch them *now*?"

Melanie shrugged hopelessly. "Go ahead if you want to. But it won't do any good. I think we might as well—leave the country, or something."

Elizabeth had followed Melanie and listened to April's horrible news. Now all of a sudden she said, "I have an idea."

Both the bigger girls looked surprised. Elizabeth wasn't the kind of person you expect to come up with ideas in an emergency. But the situation was desperate, so April and Melanie listened.

When Elizabeth finished whispering, April shook her head gloomily. "It'll never work," she said.

"Well, we may as well try it," Melanie said. "It can't make things any worse."

The enemy watched cautiously as the girls returned to face them. For a few seconds April and Melanie couldn't think of a way to get started, and the five of them just stood there staring at each other. Melanie spoke first.

"We don't have permission to be here from the Professor, or our folks or anybody."

Toby grinned. "So what else is new?" he said.

April's fists clenched but she forced herself to open them. "We'll be in terrible trouble if you tell on us," she said in as pitiful a voice as she could manage. To her amazement she noticed that the look the two boys exchanged was just the tiniest bit confused. And Kamata and Alvillar were two guys who weren't easy to confuse. Warming to her theme, she went on, "We'll probably get beaten and everything."

There was no doubt about it, the enemy had faltered for a few moments, but they managed to re-group.

"We're crying," Ken said. "See the tears."

"Yeah. We'll come to your funerals," Toby said.

Just then Elizabeth pushed her way between April and Melanie. Everyone looked at her in surprise—she'd probably never spoken to a sixth-grade boy before in her life, but now she looked as if she meant to.

"Please," she said, in a feathery little voice. "Please don't tell on us, and we'll let you play, too."

April cringed. It was such a corny, baby thing to say. She had a crazy urge to grab Elizabeth and drag her out of wisecrack range, before she got hurt. But seconds passed and nobody pounced. April unsquinched her eyes. Strangely enough, the boys were looking confused again. More confused than ever. Elizabeth was looking shyly hopeful, like an unspanked puppy.

Then Ken blinked his eyes like someone coming to after a whack on the head. "Come on, Tobe, let's get out of here," he said. And then, to no one in particular, "Maybe we won't *fink* on you guys. You never can tell. Maybe we just won't be in the mood for finking. Huh, Tobe?" But Toby only nodded absently. Ken picked up Toby's T.V. head and jammed it into his hands. "Come *on*, Tobe," he said. "We've got to get back before my dad misses me."

But Toby appeared to be thinking. He nodded again slowly and then walked around the girls to the temple. He looked for a moment at each altar and then around the yard. When he came back his eyes had a faraway look.

"Okay," he said. "Okay. We don't rat, and we get to join the game. Is it a deal?"

"Join the game!" Ken said. "This game? Are you

kidding? We could make a deal about using the yard—like for"—he paused and glanced around—"four-square or handball or something, but—" He caught a glimpse of Toby's face, and his voice trailed off. Toby was lit up like a pinball machine. Ken shrugged philosophically. "Okay," he said. "So we're Egyptians. It figures."

From then on things happened fast. Toby made everybody take a solemn oath not to tell where they'd been, even if they'd been missed and people started asking questions. Then, there was a brief crisis over getting Toby out of the yard. He wouldn't fit through the hole in the fence with his boxes on, and the big box the boys had used for climbing over was too big and heavy to throw into the yard. He couldn't take his costume off because he didn't think he could get back into it without his dad's help, and it wouldn't be wise to rejoin the trick-or-treat group in pieces. Finally he lay down on the ground and had everybody stomp on him, more or less gently (less, in the case of April, who was still mad) until the boxes were flattened enough to squeeze through the hole. Afterwards, they tried to square him back up, but he never did look quite the same.

As soon as they'd carried off the boxes the boys had piled up to climb on, they started off after the trick-or-treat group. Fortunately Ken knew the line of march, and since they didn't stop at any houses, it wasn't too long until they caught up. They even had time to collect a few more treats before it was time to go home.

But it would have taken more than a few pieces of cheap candy to console April and Melanie. After they got the two smaller kids uncostumed and sent home, they sat on April's bed and stared at each other gloomily.

"What are we going to do?" April said finally. "We just *can't* play the Egypt Game with those—those— *boys* there."

"I don't see how we can, either," Melanie said. "But what else can we do? You know what will happen if we try to keep them out. We can try to play it, anyway. Then, if they're just too awful, I guess we'll have to give the whole thing up."

It was a terrible thought. For a few minutes the two girls contemplated the possibility in mournful silence. At last, in a more cheerful voice, Melanie said, "Well, at least we don't have to give it up yet, thanks to Elizabeth. If she hadn't had that idea, I'll bet those jerks would have finked on us right away, just for the fun of it."

"Yeah," April said wonderingly. "How about that Elizabeth! How'd a little kid like that know how to handle those two creeps? I'm pretty good at handling adults and people like that, but *boys*! Yick!"

Melanie grinned. "You know? It's sort of like what you do in 'non-violence.' My mom says it's appealing to their better natures."

"Better natures, phooey!" April said, wrinkling up her nose.

Moods and Maybes

THE NEXT DAY AT RECESS TOBY ALVILLAR SIDLED UP to Melanie and April. Before he started talking, he looked around quickly to be sure no one who mattered was looking. Ken and Toby didn't believe in talking to girls. Of course, it was all right to make comments at girls—particularly if they were insults—but real conversations were out, at least in public places.

"When are you guys going 'you know where' again?" he asked, sort of out of the corner of his mouth.

"I don't know," Melanie answered. "We're not supposed to go there at all, yet. They're still not letting us play outside because of the murder and everything. But my folks are weakening, I think."

"Caroline says I can start playing outside again as soon as Melanie can," April said.

"Well, look. Ken and I won't go there until Friday," Toby said. "Try to get your folks to spring you by then. Okay?"

April and Melanie exchanged surprised glances. "Oh, we're not just being boy-scouty," Toby said. "My dad got mad at me and restricted me for three days. So I couldn't go before anyway."

April and Melanie tried not to giggle. "Yeah," Toby said. "It's all you guys' fault, too. My dad got mad at the way you guys mashed up my costume. Parents!" Toby rolled up his eyes in an exasperated expression. "All I ask him for is an *idea* for a Halloween costume. At first he says he's too busy to think about it. He's an *artist*, and he can't even think up a little old costume idea. Then, all of a sudden he gets this brainstorm and he spends a whole day making the costume, plus a couple of hours putting me into it, and then he's so hung up on the whole thing that he gets mad when I squash it a little."

April and Melanie broke down and giggled and, sure enough, Toby was encouraged. "Yeah," he said, "I just walk in the door, see, and my dad gives me this cold look and says, 'How many were killed?' I start saying what's he talking about, and he says in this icy voice, 'Well, obviously you've been hit by a truck and I was just wondering about the other casualties.' After that he got louder and not so funny—and it ends up I'm restricted for three days."

Toby mugged an exaggeratedly exasperated look again and strolled off, leaving the girls absolutely devastated with giggles. It was all very well having a rule about not laughing at Toby, but it wasn't always easy to stick to it.

That night at home Melanie brought up the subject of playing outdoors and got her parents started on an argument about it. Her father's opinion was that "we can't keep them cooped up forever," and fortunately he won—on the condition that Marshall and Melanie promise not to play alone. So it all had to wait until the Rosses could get around to talking with Mrs. Hall and Mrs. Chung and get everything all decided—and by then it was already Thursday.

On Thursday afternoon the three girls picked up Marshall at his nursery school and hurried to Egypt. They had just one day to spend there in peace and quiet before the coming of the "outsiders." It was a nice sunny afternoon and everything was right where they'd left it, but somehow it was hard to keep their minds on the Game. They were all worrying about the next day. They were wondering if the boys really wanted to play, or if they just wanted to tease and make trouble. April said it wouldn't surprise her a bit if they showed up with half the boys in the sixth grade and just smashed everything to pieces. In fact, April said she thought they might just as well give the whole thing up and go away and never come back.

Later Elizabeth, with worried wrinkles in her forehead, asked Melanie if April really meant it. Were they really going to give up the Egypt Game? But Melanie told her not to worry. "She doesn't mean it," Melanie said. "She's just in a bad mood about something. Can't you tell?"

And April was in a bad mood. She had been in a bad mood since the day before, when she'd gotten a letter from Hollywood. The letter was from Dorothea, and it was very cheery and chatty—and it said that Dorothea and Nick had gotten married. Dorothea chatted about how happy she and Nick were, and how she'd moved into Nick's apartment and there really wasn't much room. "Of course," the letter said, "we're both looking forward just awfully to the time when we can get more settled and have a bigger place and have you come to live with us. But in the meantime, darling, I'm sending the rest of your things on up to Caroline's as the storage situation here is just terrible."

There was a lot more about the big part that Dorothea was about to get—not the same one as she'd written about last time, which hadn't really been her type of thing, anyway. But this new part—

April hadn't finished the letter. She had torn it up

into little tiny pieces and flushed it down the toilet, so she couldn't change her mind and paste it back together. Then she sat on the windowsill and stared off up Orchard Avenue. She had still been sitting there when Caroline came in, but April hadn't turned around.

"I got a letter from your mother today, too, dear," Caroline had said. She put one hand very gently on April's shoulder.

Hot tears had drowned April's eyes and painful gulps climbed up her throat. She had hated the hand on her shoulder and she had hated Caroline because it was all her fault. She'd been all right until Caroline came in—just angry. *Mad—mad—mad*, but all right. And then Caroline had to come in and make her cry.

Caroline had just stood there, and once or twice she had made a little sound in her throat as if she were going to say something, but she never did. After a while the painful gulps wore themselves out and the tears running down April's cheeks began to feel almost good, soothing like warm rain. Suddenly she had felt empty and very tired, and because she was so tired she let her head lean over towards Caroline just a little bit—not really touching, but almost. They stayed that way for quite a while and then Caroline had given April's shoulder a squeeze, kissed her quickly on top of the head and gone out.

April had sat there a while longer, tasting the tears

on her face with the tip of her tongue and thinking how long it had been since she'd cried enough to taste. And thinking, too, that a kiss on top of the head was okay, and didn't make you want to rub it off the way a kiss on the cheek did. Things were better after that but April had gone on being in a bad mood.

Melanie didn't know about the letter, but she knew something was wrong, and she was worried. Friday afternoon was going to be difficult enough without April's being in one of her touchy moods. But by Friday, April was in a much better frame of mind. Melanie could tell that she had gotten her mind off whatever it had been that was bothering her because she started making cheerful plans in school about getting the best of Ken and Toby.

That afternoon the girls and Marshall got to the storage yard first, and they were all sitting on the edge of the temple floor just waiting when Ken and Toby arrived. Ken had to do a certain amount of squeezing and inhaling to get through the fence, but skinny Toby came through almost as easily as the girls, now that he wasn't wearing boxes. They didn't say much at first, just "Hi," and then the boys started looking around at the altars and the things on them. The girls watched warily, trying to figure out just what they had in mind.

After a few minutes Melanie decided that Ken really didn't have anything in mind at all. He looked reluctant and puzzled and a little bit embarrassed. She decided that Ken was only there because Toby was, so she started watching Toby.

It was easy to tell by looking at Toby's dark eyes that something important was going on behind them. They almost gave you the feeling that you could hear things inside his head going "whirr-clank-buzz," but for once it didn't seem to have anything to do with laughter. Melanie began to get the feeling that maybe Toby wasn't just there to tease and cut up after all.

So when Toby started asking questions about the things on the altars and about Set and Isis, Melanie started giving straight answers. At first April poked her and frowned in a way that said not to give everything away, but after a while she changed her mind and started answering questions, too. She even took the secret scrolls out of their hiding place in the hollow base of the statue of Diana and showed the boys the list of things to do for different ceremonies and the partly finished hieroglyphic alphabet. Finally Toby left the shed and walked to the middle of the yard.

Ken looked relieved. "Well, I guess that's all there is to see," he said to Toby. "We might as well split, huh? We'll still have time to get in the game up at school."

But Toby shook his head. "I don't feel like playing basketball," he said. "Besides, I sort of go for this Egypt stuff. Let's hang around awhile. Okay?"

Ken shrugged. "Sheesh!" he said. "I don't care. But the whole scene's pretty kooky, if you ask me."

It turned out that Toby wasn't kidding—he really did go for the Egypt Game. He wanted to hear and see everything, and that first afternoon he somehow managed to talk the girl Egyptians into doing all their ceremonies and rituals over for him to watch. At first they were still a little suspicious and embarrassed, but when it became clear that he wasn't going to tease they became more enthusiastic. A couple of times he even made approving comments like, "Hey! Weird!" or, "Holy cow."

Ken was pretty respectful about the whole thing, too. He kept hitting himself on the forehead and saying "Sheesh!" but his tone of voice seemed to indicate amazement more than anything else.

As they were all leaving, a little before 5:30, Toby asked the girls to write down the names of some of the best books about Egypt. He said he was going to the library that evening to check some out.

That night April and Melanie sat on Melanie's bed and, feeling very pleased with things in general, they discussed the future. The first meeting of the enlarged Egypt gang had gone off much more smoothly than they had expected. They didn't admit it, even to each other, but they had both been flattered by Ken's and Toby's respectful interest.

"And maybe, after a week or two, they'll lose interest," Melanie said. "Maybe they'll play for a while and then they'll get homesick for their old ball games, and everything will be just like it used to be."

"Yeah," April agreed. "I'll bet they do. Or else, maybe they won't even come back at all. Maybe they were just curious, and now that they know all about it, they just might not bother to come back. And I don't think they're going to fink to the other kids, either. At least, not as long as they don't get mad at us, or something. You know, I wouldn't be surprised if they just don't show up tomorrow at all."

Hieroglyphics

KEN AND TOBY SHOWED UP IN EGYPT THE NEXT DAY, all right. They showed up right on time, overflowing with ideas and loaded down with stuff. At least, Toby was overflowing with ideas, and Ken was carrying most of the stuff.

The four original Egyptians were especially thrilled and amazed about the stuff the boys brought for Set. It seemed that sixth-grade boys just normally kept a lot of things around that were perfect for the altar of an evil god. Set's altar, which had always been rather bare in comparison to Isis's jeweled and flowered throne, was suddenly rich with ornaments. There were several lifelike rubber things—spiders, snakes and bugs. There was a real skull of a medium-size animal, maybe a cat or a skunk, and a well-preserved dead tarantula. There was a wicked-looking theatrical dagger, with a twisted blade that sank into the handle to make fake stabbings look real. But the two best things were a shrunken head and a large stuffed owl.

The shrunken head wasn't real, of course, but it was an expensive rubber one that did look terribly real. It was Ken's, and he was obviously quite pleased with himself for bringing it. The owl was Toby's and it was real; that is, it had been once, but now it was stuffed. It was a little beat-up-looking, but Toby said that was because he'd had it ever since he was a baby. Actually, what he said was that his father had given it to him to cut his teeth on when he was five months old, but that might only have been one of Toby's stories.

Anyway, it looked great perched on a little shelf just above the altar of the evil god. It sat there, in the shadows among the spiderwebs, and peered down balefully over its tooth-scarred beak. At first Toby suggested that it could be a servant of Set, whose duty was to carry the message of doom to Set's victims; but later on someone remembered Thoth, the bird-headed god of wisdom and writing. From then on the owl was known as Thoth.

Besides all the other stuff, Toby had also brought some pencils and paper. He said he'd been thinking it over, and he'd decided the first thing they ought to do was finish the alphabet of hieroglyphics the girls had started.

"Oh, is that right," April said. "Is that what you've decided? Whose Egypt Game do you think this is, anyway? Just because—"

She had a lot more things to say, but Toby interrupted. "Okay, okay. Cool it for a minute and let me finish. Let me tell you the rest of my idea before you start coming unglued. Then if you don't buy it—" he shrugged—"we won't do it."

That seemed fair enough, so April shut up, but she kept her eyes narrowed warily as Toby explained. When they had the alphabet all made up, they could memorize it and use it to write secret messages—at school and everyplace. They could write about things like when to meet in Egypt again, and what they thought of the teacher, and all sorts of other private information. Then if the messages fell into enemy hands, no one would know what it was all about. Besides that, Toby thought they should each choose an Egyptian name—Marshall was already Marshamosis—and a hieroglyphic symbol that stood for the name. That way each one could sign his messages with his symbol and that would make the whole thing more mysterious. Toby took out a piece of paper all folded up into a tiny square and spread it out on the floor of the shed. On it were some hieroglyphics and some Egyptian names that he had copied out of books the night before. Everyone except April immediately got down on hands and knees and began to examine the paper eagerly and discuss possible names.

April was telling herself it was a crummy idea, when all of a sudden she remembered Bastet. Bastet had always seemed especially intriguing to April. She was a sort of cat goddess, and there was a famous statue of her as a cat, with cruel mysterious eyes and earrings in her ears. If you were to pick the name of Bastet, your symbol could be a cat's head with earrings. "Hey," she said, dropping down to join the group, "I've got a great one."

Everybody liked April's name and hieroglyph. In fact, Toby said it gave him an idea for a hieroglyph for himself. He'd already picked out his name. It was going to be Ramose, after a famous Egyptian wise man. And since an owl was supposed to be wise, what could be better than an owl's head for a symbol?

Melanie knew right away what she wanted her name to be. She had gone once with her parents to hear Grace Bumbry sing *Aïda* and had been fascinated with the tragic story of the beautiful princess who had been a captive in ancient Egypt. As a matter of fact, she'd already thought of herself as Aïda, at times, when they were playing the Egypt Game, but she hadn't told anyone. A symbol to go with Aïda was a bit of a problem, but finally Melanie picked the

TOP SECRET
MEMBERS of EGYPT GAME

Toby RAMOSE

Ken HOREMNEB

Melanie AIDA

April BASTET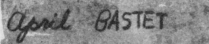

Elizabeth NEFERTITI
(NEFERBETH)

Marshall MARSHAMOSIS

bird hieroglyph because it stood for the letter A in the real Egyptian alphabet.

When everyone was through choosing, Melanie made a new scroll and added it to the secret records.

Ken had picked the name of Horemheb because Toby said Horemheb had been a great general and also a pharaoh. He thought up his own hieroglyph of a bloody sword. There wasn't anything particularly Egyptian about it, but it did seem to go with being a general. Elizabeth's symbol was April's idea. It was a real Egyptian hieroglyph and it meant "heart," to go with Nefertiti, which means "Beloved One." And of course Marshall's hieroglyph was the double crown of Egypt because he was already the boy-pharaoh—and that's what he liked to be best.

The next few meetings of the Egyptians were taken up with finishing the hieroglyphic alphabet and memorizing it. Some of the letters that they used in their alphabet were actual Egyptian hieroglyphs, but for the sounds that were missing in the Egyptian alphabet, as well as a few that were too difficult to draw in their original form, they made up their own. Then, because their book on Egyptian writing told how hieroglyphics were considered magical works of art as well as writing, and because they were always done in many bright colors, it was decided that some sets of colored pens were necessary. So the game was suspended for a couple of afternoons while money was raised to buy the pens. Ken and Toby mowed a few lawns, and the girls and Marshall scouted the neighborhood for empty bottles to return to the grocery store.

Just buying the pens took most of another afternoon because it took so long to get waited on at Schmitt's Variety Store. Melanie said her mother said that the reason Mr. Schmitt never had a clerk for long was that he paid such low salaries. Except for Mr. Schmitt's cousin, a stocky redheaded young man with blotchy freckles, there was no one working in the store that day but Mr. Schmitt. The cousin never waited on customers, but only dusted shelves and brought stuff out from the back room; and Mr. Schmitt, himself, never waited on kids until after all the grown-ups were taken care of, no matter who'd been there longest. So the Egypt gang waited and waited and it was all pretty frustrating.

But the pens were worth the effort, and during the next few days Egypt was full of scribes practicing the ancient art of hieroglyphic writing. In a short time all sorts of possibilities were suggested and explored. Letters were written and exchanged and deciphered. Decorative hieroglyphic borders were added to the poster-paint pictures that already adorned the walls of the temple. Secret mailing spots were picked out all around the neighborhood, such as a certain clump of weeds in an untended parkway or the crotch of a particular plum tree. A mysterious and beautifully drawn page of hieroglyphics got loose in the sixth-grade class at Wilson School and was passed around and puzzled over by everyone, including the teacher; but no one came even close to figuring it out. And of course, no one was as loudly and dramatically puzzled as the four sixth-grade members of the Egypt Game.

Later, there was a brief and bloodless war, a sort of battle of the scribes, when Ramose and Bastet started an argument over whether a line of hieroglyphics should be written from left to right or from up to down. Everybody took sides and went home mad; and for a day or two Toby and Ken went back to playing basketball after school.

It turned out to be a good thing really, because they were just in time to find out about a plot. Some of the other boys had gotten so curious about what Ken and Toby had found to do after school that was better than basketball, that they were getting ready to launch an investigation.

Toby took care of that in a hurry. Without exactly saying so, he managed to spread the rumor that he and Ken had an after-school job—a very serious job involving actual work. Toby figured that there was nothing less interesting to most of the kids he knew than an after-school job, and he was right. After that the other boys weren't nearly so curious.

Then when a few days had passed and all the Egyptians had had a chance to cool off, Ken and Toby turned up in Egypt again—and the others were glad to see them. It did seem best not to talk about hieroglyphics right away—but that was all right because everyone was a little tired of them anyhow—particularly Marshall.

It wasn't that Marshall hadn't taken any interest in hieroglyphic writing, because he had. As a matter of fact, he could almost do a better job of reading and writing in Egyptian than he could in English. But, since he wasn't even in kindergarten yet, he wasn't exactly fluent in either one. So towards the end of the hieroglyphic period, when he'd learned about as much Egyptian writing as he felt ready for, he hadn't had very much to do. Most of the time he spent just watching. He had watched the other Egyptians writing and planning and arguing, he had watched an ant hole in the corner of the storage yard, and every once in a while he had watched the little window in one of the walls of the land of Egypt.

Then, one day not long after Ken and Toby returned to the land of Egypt, a neighbor's cat got into the Chungs' apartment and killed Petey the parakeet —the only pet Elizabeth had ever owned. Elizabeth was brokenhearted, and it was while they were trying to cheer her up that April and Melanie got the idea for the Ceremony for the Dead.

The Ceremony for the Dead

IT WAS SATURDAY AFTERNOON AND APRIL, MELANIE and Marshall had just come down to get Elizabeth to join the boys in Egypt for a previously scheduled rendezvous. When Elizabeth met them at the door with her dead pet, and tears in her eyes, it was only natural that somebody should think of a funeral. And when April and Melanie started tossing the idea back and forth, decorating and elaborating the way they always did, it worked just the way it was supposed to. Elizabeth's tears slowed up, and a damp dimple flickered in her cheek.

By the time the three girls and Marshall squeezed through the fence to Egypt, where Ken and Toby were already waiting, a great deal of the necessary background material was already beginning to take shape. Prince Pete-ho-tep, son of the great Queen

Neferbeth, had just fallen in a battle with a terrible monster, and his body was being taken in solemn procession to the temple of Anubis, God of the Dead.

Ken and Toby were gratifyingly enthusiastic. In fact, Toby, who always had to be right in the middle of everything, insisted right away that he and Ken—Horemheb, that is—were going to be the high priests of Anubis.

"Now, just a minute," April said. "Melanie and I thought up this ceremony. We get to be the high priestesses of the dead."

"You mean Aïda—you and Aïda," Toby corrected. Just the day before a rule had been passed that members should be called only by their Egyptian names while they were inside the land of Egypt.

"Okay! Me and Aïda. Anyway it was our idea."

"Yeah, but I've just finished reading a great book that tells all about what they did to the mummies and everything. I've got some tough ideas."

"So have I," April said.

"Queen Neferbeth ought to choose the high priest," Melanie said, interrupting the exchange of glares. "After all, it's her parakeet."

That broke the deadlock. Elizabeth didn't want to decide against anybody, so she put a pebble in one hand and let them choose. Ken and Toby won and got to be the high priests of Anubis.

The first thing Toby did as high priest was to

announce that the whole thing was going to take a long time. In real Egyptian times, he said, the preparation of the dead and the funeral ceremony took as much as forty days. Theirs wouldn't take that long, but maybe it would last as much as five or six. He said that before he could really get started, they were going to need a lot of supplies, so until he could get the things he needed they might just as well go on with the procession to the temple.

Melanie suggested that the procession needed palm branches and flower petals and that sort of thing; and of course everyone thought of the trash bin behind the florist shop. So, a few minutes later, the entire population of Egypt was sneaking up the alley on the way to sort over the florist's recent rejects. As soon as they returned, loaded with loot, the procession got under way.

Marshall came first, carrying the smoking incense burner. Next came Elizabeth, as the Queen Mother and Chief Mourner. One of the curtain robes was draped over her head as a veil and she carried a big bouquet of only slightly wilted dahlias. Then came April and Melanie as the mourning populace, scattering flowers and chanting, "Weep for Prince Pete-ho-tep—fallen in battle," in a high mournful wail. And last of all came the two high priests of Anubis, carrying on a flower-strewn plank the dead body of Prince Pete-ho-tep.

The procession wound its way back and forth across the storage yard several times, and came to a stop in the temple. There the bier was placed on a specially prepared altar in the middle of the floor. At that point the ceremony had to stop for fresh ideas. Since this was the first Ceremony for the Dead there was no record scroll to follow, and it was necessary to stop now and then for discussion and new suggestions. Afterwards, of course, Melanie would make a record of the things that were done—and any future Ceremony for the Dead wouldn't have to stop and start.

All the other ceremonies and rites had been developed in the same way, but this time there was a difference. This was the first new ceremony to be made up since the coming of the two new Egyptians, and the first real ceremony they'd actually taken part in. April and Melanie had often wondered if they ever really would.

But they needn't have wondered. The boys took part, all right, and to an extent that nobody had expected. For instance, it was Toby who suggested that they march around the altar, beating their chests and sprinkling their heads with ashes and wailing. That wasn't so much of a surprise. He'd already demonstrated that he had lots of good ideas. It was the way he threw himself into the part that came as a shock to the girls. He was so different from what he was at school. At school he was Toby the cool-cat sophisticate; and now, suddenly, he was Toby, the grief-stricken ancient Egyptian. And, somehow, he gave the feeling there were a lot of other roles he could play just as well.

Ken was a different matter, although he, too, did a lot better than anybody would have expected. He was, of course, absolutely perfect at being himself, and he was very much at home in the role. But this Egyptian business was something else again.

And so, while Toby staggered around the altar, beating his chest with wild-eyed abandon, sprinkling real ashes—left over from Set's sacrificial fire—in his hair, and wailing like a wounded electric guitar; and while, right behind him, April and Melanie did more or less the same things, just about as realistically, except they were using imaginary ashes—because to a girl even the death of a pharaoh isn't worth a dirty head; and while Elizabeth did everything April and

Melanie did, only softer; and while even Marshall marched with solemn assurance, thumping his chest firmly with the hand that wasn't holding Security, and making a noise like a stuck recording, Ken brought up the rear.

If the rest of them could do it, Ken Kamata could, too, and he did. But it wasn't easy. Every time he thumped his chest or made a brief, halfhearted wail, he felt his ears get hot; and from time to time he announced to nobody in particular, "Sheesh! I feel like a kook."

When 5:30 came and everyone was leaving, Toby told the other members of the Egypt Game to call him up that evening and he would assign them something to bring. He was going to do some research, he said, to find out exactly what was needed to make a mummy. But there was an awful lot to learn about mummies, and even after a whole evening of study it turned out that Toby's information wasn't all that complete. For instance, when Ken, who was assigned to bring oil, wanted to know what kind, Toby couldn't exactly say. It didn't seem likely that the ancient Egyptians used any of the kinds Ken and Toby knew about—crankcase, sewing machine, polyunsaturated or bicycle. They finally settled for bicycle, because oil was oil, and bicycle was the only kind that Ken owned personally.

When the Egyptians had assembled the next afternoon, bringing their offerings of oil and spice and salt and perfume, Toby—Ramose—gave a little talk on how to prepare a mummy. It was a good speech, but it suffered from frequent interruptions because Bastet and Aïda had read the same book and had some ideas of their own. And there was another pause while everyone tried to comfort Queen Neferbeth, who got all upset when Ramose spoke indelicately about "taking out the guts." It turned out that Queen Neferbeth felt so strongly about "cutting holes in Petey," even if he was dead, that it was decided to dispense with that part of the procedure.

"It'll be all right, Tobe—uh—Ramose," Horemheb said. "He's so little he can't have enough guts to make that much difference."

Toby was disappointed, but he had to admit that according to the book there was another way. Poor people, who couldn't afford the more expensive process, had been simply soaked in brine.

So the rest of the afternoon was taken up in preparing a saltwater bath for Prince Pete-ho-tep and placing him in it with the proper pomp. Then he was left to soak.

The appearance of the mummy-to-be when he was removed from his brine bath, on the following afternoon, was something of a shock to everybody. His wet feathers stuck to his tiny body and he was covered with a thick white salty scum. When Toby lifted him gingerly out of the brine by one claw, everybody felt a little queasy, and Elizabeth's eyes became suspiciously liquid.

Toby glanced at her and sighed impatiently. "Now just cool it a minute, Neferbeth," he said. "I'll have him all fixed up in two seconds." He hastily poured some fresh water over the parakeet and dried him off on the tail of his T-shirt, which was huge and dingy and probably belonged to his father.

When Pete-ho-tep was dry and his feathers rearranged, he did look almost as good as new, and the mummification process continued. In the next few days he was anointed with spices and perfume, wrapped in thin strips of oil-soaked cloth, and laid to rest with a supply of birdseed and a few of his favorite toys, in a smallish pyramid made of old bricks.

It was a good week in the land of Egypt. Melanie collected several new ceremonies to add to the sacred records; Ken began to find being an ancient Egyptian a little less embarrassing; and Elizabeth felt so proud of the important part that Petey had played, she almost forgot how much she missed him.

But as the Egypt Game became second nature to its six participants, and they began to feel more and more at home in the land of Egypt, they gradually began to forget about being cautious. Ceremonies, discussions and arguments began to be carried on in normal or even louder than normal tones and no one stopped to worry about being overheard. Only one very small Egyptian had an idea that the land of Egypt was being watched, and for some reason, which was his own and private, he didn't choose to tell.

The Oracle of Thoth

STRANGE AS IT MAY SEEM, MRS. GRANGER, THE SIXTH-grade teacher at Wilson, was responsible for the next phase of the Egypt Game. It all grew out of the fact that an assignment the class was reading just barely mentioned something called an oracle. Toby had a pretty good idea of what an oracle was but he decided to ask Mrs. Granger about it, in the hopes of getting her started on one of her long-winded explanations. A test was scheduled for the end of the period, and Mrs. Granger had been known to forget about such things, if you handled it just right.

So Toby asked a question about oracles and sure enough it worked. He'd picked on a subject that Mrs. Granger could really get her teeth into. She got that gleam in her eye and started out full blast, and Toby settled back, feeling sure she was good for the rest of the time until recess.

But the way it turned out, the whole thing sort of backfired, because by the end of the period the whole class—Toby included—was as hung up on the whole oracle bit as Mrs. Granger was. As a matter of fact, it had completely slipped Toby's mind that he'd only asked about it to head off a test. Mrs. Granger could do that sort of thing to you, if you weren't careful.

During library period, which came next, a lot of people got stuff to read about oracles, and that afternoon there was another discussion in class. Everyone had come up with a lot of info about the different kinds of oracles and how they predicted the future in different ways—through the actions of sacred snakes or birds or fish or even through the way the insides of a dead animal were arranged when the priests cut it open. There was even one very famous one that was run by a priestess who went into a kind of trance or fit, and while she was clear off in this trance she spouted out a lot of messages and stuff that were supposed to come right straight from the mouths of the gods. The oracles all had special sacred places, caves or grottoes or specially built temples, and there were all sorts of far-out things connected with them like sacred fires and mystic vapors and magical statues.

Among the stuff reported to the class was a list of

the countries that had depended on oracles to help the rulers decide how to run things. And one of the countries was Egypt.

As soon as he heard it, Toby remembered reading something about the Egyptian priests making predictions, but he just hadn't been thinking about the oracles in connection with the Egypt Game until that moment. He snuck a glance in the direction of Ross and February, to see if they had the same idea, and sure enough, they had. It was easy to tell. They were staring at each other in that way they had. If they were where they could talk, Toby thought to himself, one of them would be starting a sentence and the other finishing it—as if they had Siamese brains, or something. Just at that moment the girls stopped staring at each other and turned and stared at Toby.

They were giving him that same bit with the eyes that they used on each other; and if he'd wanted to, Toby could have given it right back. He knew what they were saying, all right. Instead, he slowly and deliberately made his eyes go crossed and let his mouth fall open in a "stupid-idiot" face.

The reaction was just what he'd expected. The girls looked shocked, then angry, and then they turned their backs and worked hard at ignoring him for the rest of the period. Toby let his mind go back to his plans for the afternoon with a feeling of satisfaction.

They would have forgotten about being mad by the time school was out—and besides, they'd really asked for it. He'd told those girls before, Egypt was Egypt, but at school you had to play it cool.

That afternoon's two hours in Egypt turned out to be mostly a long discussion of the What and How of the Egyptian Oracle. April had her mind set on the kind of oracle that got its messages from the gods through a high priestess with fits. And, naturally, she was all set to be the high priestess. She would sit on a throne before the sacred fire, surrounded by swirling mystic vapors, and people who wanted predictions would write their question on a slip of paper and drop it in the fire. She would go into a trance, and *then* she would speak with the voice of the gods.

That was just great as far as the trance was concerned, Toby thought. If anybody could throw a far-out fit, April could. And if he hadn't cooked up such a great idea himself, he'd have been tempted to go along with April's version just to see how she'd do it. But the fact of the matter was, he had a scheme that was going to make the oracle bit just about the greatest thing that had ever hit the land of Egypt. So, much as he hated to do it, he set about spoiling April's plans.

"So, when they drop their questions in the fire," he asked, "how are you going to know what to answer? Particularly if you haven't even seen the question?"

"You must not have been listening in class today," April said. "*I* don't have to know. The gods speak through the mouth of the priestess." Sometimes it was hard to tell whether April was kidding or whether she really believed stuff like that.

Ken was looking at April in consternation. "You really think the gods are . . ." His voice faded away and for a minute he just stared at April. "Sheesh!" he said at last. "You really are cracking up this time."

But Toby only raised an eyebrow and gave April his cool-amusement look. "Sure," he said, "but don't you think we ought to have something else planned? Just in case the gods don't get the message."

Then, while April glared at him, Toby told everybody *his* idea, and naturally everybody thought it was the greatest. Even April, after she'd had a chance to cool off. The way Toby saw it, somebody would think up a question they wanted answered about the future. Then they would write it on a piece of paper and bring the paper to the temple of the oracle. At the temple the priest—or priestess, he added graciously—would pass the paper over the sacred fire, and do whatever other stuff he could think up. Then—and this was the good part—he would take it to this special altar they would build for Thoth and put the question in his beak and leave it there overnight.

Toby jumped up and grabbed Thoth down off the shelf and dusted him off. "After all," Toby said, "Thoth was the *Egyptian* god of wisdom, and this crazy priestess bit was something the Greeks thought up."

That was a good point, and after that there wasn't much more argument—except that April did say if they were going to be so particular, how about the fact that actually Thoth was supposed to be an ibis and not an old chewed-up owl. But nobody paid much attention to her. They were all too busy starting in on Thoth's altar and planning the ceremony for Consulting the Oracle.

It was decided that they would draw straws and the winner would get to be the first one to ask the oracle a question. They gave the straws to Marshall to hold and everybody drew. And, just as you'd think, the winner was Ken, the one guy who really didn't want to win.

"Sheesh," Ken said. "I don't know anything to ask. Anything I can't find out for myself, I don't even want to know."

"Now look," Toby said. "You won and you can't cop out on it. That's poor sportsmanship. Anybody can think of a little old question about the future. I'll bet even Marshall could think up a lot of questions, and he's only four years old."

"I can think up three bags full," Marshall said.

Nobody ever got away with calling Ken a poor sportsman. His chin got the hard look it got just before he slammed a home run, and after a minute you could tell he'd thought of something because his ears got red. "Okay," he said, "I got a question. Give me the paper."

At that point, Melanie suggested that perhaps the questions to the oracle ought to be written in hieroglyphics, but for some reason Toby was against it. As soon as Ken had written his question, Toby grabbed the folded paper, and, stepping up to the new altar, he started right in being the priest of the oracle. By the time a certain party realized what had happened, she was too interested in what was going on to argue.

Toby pressed the slip of paper to his forehead and walked three times around the temple. Then he made Ken kneel before the altar of Thoth and press the paper to Thoth's forehead, while Toby sprinkled them both with holy water from the tuna can. Next he hung the paper on one of Thoth's long sharp toenails and sprinkled it with more holy water. Finally he waved it back and forth in the smoke from the incense burner, chanting, "Hear us, O Thoth, ancient and wise. Hear us and answer."

There was no doubt about it, Toby made a great high priest. The other Egyptians were so caught up in his smooth solemnity and exalted priestly expression that they found themselves almost believing—well, half-believing—that Toby was actually talking to an ancient and powerful being, and that something strange and supernatural was about to happen. So, when Toby turned to them a moment later and thundered, "Kneel and bow low—O ancient Egyptians—before the miracle of the oracle!" they hurried to obey.

A moment later, when they lifted their foreheads from the temple floor, the scrap of paper was hanging in Thoth's curved beak, and Toby was backing away from the altar, bowing at every step.

When Toby had backed to where the others were kneeling, he got them up and hustled them out of the temple. Out in the middle of the storage yard, he dropped his high-priest expression. In his normal voice he said, "Well, I guess we might as well cut out. If we hang around, somebody's going to read what's on Ken's question before tomorrow and that would ruin everything."

April's eyes flattened. "Like what for instance?" she asked. "Just what do you have in mind that might get ruined, Mr. Oracle?"

"Have in mind?" Toby said, giving her the wide-eyed-innocence treatment. "*I* don't have anything in mind. It's just that I don't want anybody else to either. At least, not until we find out what the oracle can do all by itself."

"Wait a *minute*, Tobe!" Ken said, looking worried again. "You don't mean *you* think there's a chance it might? How about what you said before—about the gods not getting the message and all that? Sheesh! Sometimes I think the whole bunch of you guys are going off your rockers."

Toby gave Ken a reassuring grin. "Cool it," he said. "I don't think anything. At least not anything for sure. I just think we ought to give it a chance. Then if nothing happens, we can take turns being the one who makes up the answers. But what I do think is, you never can tell about a thing like this." He lowered his voice mysteriously. "After all, it *used* to work, didn't it? I mean all those other oracles weren't just kid stuff. Even kings and generals and all sorts of other adults used to go for this oracle stuff, didn't they? Well—"

As one person, the six Egyptians turned and looked back into the temple-shed. The sun was very low and the shade was deep in the back of the temple where the new altar to Thoth had been built. The huge tattered owl seemed to be leaning forward, staring into the incense burner; and as they watched, a final twist of fragrant smoke curled upward like a dancing snake and seemed to wind itself around the head of Thoth.

Someone moved towards the opening in the fence, and the other five followed so quickly that it was almost as if nobody much wanted to be the last one out into the alley.

The Oracle Speaks

THE NEXT DAY, BY PREARRANGEMENT, ALL THE
Egyptians met in the alley and entered the land of
Egypt together. Toby said that was necessary so no
one would have a chance to fool around with the
oracle before everyone was there. Once inside the
yard, everyone looked at Toby, but Toby looked at
April.

"Okay, Bastet," he said, "you wanted to be the oracle priestess, so today it's your turn. You can do the
Ceremony of Returning to the Oracle for the Answer.
That is, unless you don't think you can think up a
good answer."

"I can think of answers to anything," April said.
"But I thought you were expecting the oracle to do its
own answers. Or did you change your mind?"

"Oh no," Toby said. "I didn't change my mind.

I just thought you ought to have some good answers ready, just in case. So, let's get going."

So April took charge. To get everyone in the mood, she got the box of costumes out of the shed and had everyone put something on, a headdress or a robe or at least some jewelry. Then she set the scene. "Okay," she said, "Horemheb, the famous general, has come on a pilgrimage to the grotto of the Oracle of Thoth to ask a terribly important question. He arrived at the grotto a few days ago and asked his question, and since then he has been fasting in a holy cell while he waits for the answer. You know, people who were going to the oracle had to prepare themselves very carefully, so they usually shut themselves up for days without any food and meditated until they felt very pure and sort of dizzy, and then they were ready to go. So that's what you've been doing, Ken."

Ken looked self-conscious, and Melanie made a funny, smothered sound. April was careful not to catch her eye. She knew that Melanie was trying not to laugh at the idea of solid old Ken being "pure and dizzy." April hurried on.

"The rest of us are priests and attendants of the Oracle. And I'm the high priestess who is the only one who can go into the altar room where the oracle gives out the answers."

Next, April had everyone help make some twisted paper logs to burn in the sacred fire-bowl, and then she lined them all up for a procession to the grotto. Ken was in the middle in the place of honor and April demonstrated to him how he should walk—with his hands crossed over his chest and his eyes sort of rolled up. April herself led the procession; and when they had gone twice around the yard, she lined everyone up on the edge of the temple. Then she approached the altar alone.

First she lit the candles and the incense and the sacred fire, and put the fire-bowl on the floor in front of the altar. On the altar, Thoth still sat with the slip of paper in his beak, exactly as they'd left him the night before. April bowed low before him and started in on an elaborate ceremony, using some of the old things they'd done before and some new ones she'd just thought up. She walked around the altar backwards three times sprinkling holy water. She pulled out three hairs from her head and dropped them on the fire. Then she sat down cross-legged between the fire and the altar and began to chant. Melanie sat down, too, on the edge of the temple floor and motioned for the others to do the same.

"Aie-ie-ie-ie!" April chanted, making her voice go up and down the scale; and along the edge of the temple, the other Egyptians took it up. When the wailing chant was going strong, April suddenly cried, "Stop! The mighty Thoth has heard us. The oracle has spoken!"

Very slowly and dramatically, with her eyes half closed and her face smoothed into a dream-like calmness, April raised her arms above her head and with both hands took the message from the beak of Thoth. Very, very slowly she brought it down to eye level and unfolded it. She read it carefully and then turned it over and read the other side. Her calmly regal high-priestess expression faded and she frowned as she read each side again. Then she stood up and stomped out of the temple. The rest of the Egyptians jumped up.

"Okay," April said. "Who's the wise guy?"

"Wise guy?"

"What's the matter?"

"What does it say?"

Everybody was talking at once.

"What did you write on this paper yesterday?" April asked Ken. "What was your question?"

Ken shrugged. "Oh, I don't know," he said. "Just some dumb stuff about if I was going to be a star in the big leagues some day."

April held out the slip of paper and everybody crowded around to look. In Ken's large neat handwriting it said:

Will I be a big league star someday?

"Yeah, that's it," Ken said. "That's what I wrote."

But then April turned the paper over so the other side was visible. In a very different handwriting, small and jittery, there was written:

Man is his own star, and that soul who can be honest, is the only perfect man.

"How about that?" April asked. "Did you write that too?"

"Me?" Ken said in amazement. "No way! I didn't have time to write all that. Besides, I don't even know what it means."

April and Melanie looked at each other and nodded. It was true—it didn't sound like anything Ken would do. They turned to Toby.

"Okay, Toby," April said. "When did you write this?"

Toby looked disgusted. "Let's not get ridiculous," he said. "How could I have written all that without anybody seeing me?"

"Well, you must have," April said, "because I know none of the rest of us did it."

"Oh yeah?" Toby said. "I'll bet you did it yourself."

From there on the argument began to get louder and more personal. There were accusations and counteraccusations, but no one would admit to writing the mysterious and puzzling words that straggled across the back of Ken's question. It was finally Melanie who made peace by suggesting that maybe they should just try the whole thing again and see what happened, instead of fighting about it. "We can watch to see that nobody writes an answer, and then if we get another answer and we *know* none of us wrote it . . ." Her voice trailed off and nobody offered to finish the sentence for her. It was the kind of thought that isn't easily finished.

It was April who won the straw drawing this time, and she thought quite a while before she decided on a question. After she had written it on a piece of notebook paper, she showed everyone the clean clear back of the paper before she handed it, folded, to Toby for the Ceremony of Presenting the Question to the Oracle. Toby presided again as the high priest, and his ceremony was almost exactly the same as the day before.

That is, the things Toby did were just about the same, but somehow the feeling was different. Or perhaps, not so much different as more so. More spooky and supernatural. Even though all the Egyptians were positive that somebody was fooling and had somehow managed to write the answer to Ken's question, there are times when being positive isn't quite enough.

There wasn't much light in the land of Egypt that afternoon, which didn't make it all less strange. The days had been getting shorter, of course, but it was something more than a gradual seasonal change. As Toby bowed and mumbled and chanted before the altar of Thoth, his high-priest face looking distant and unfamiliar in the deep shadow and flickering candlelight, low black clouds were moving in swiftly from the bay. In the temple it was suddenly so dark that the reflected candles lit Thoth's glassy stare with points of fire.

Then, just as Toby was finishing his ceremony, there was a huge shuddering thumping-noise that seemed to come from everywhere at once. Elizabeth gave a little scream and everyone rushed out of the temple. It wasn't until a rain-filled blast of air swept into the land of Egypt a moment later that the noise was recognized for what it was.

"Thunder! That was thunder!" everybody started saying to each other in voices that were giggly with relief. Somehow, without quite knowing how they'd gotten there, they were all six standing in a rather tight little group in the center of the storage yard.

"And rain! Wow!" somebody added.

That was the day they found out that it really *was* impossible for more than one person at a time to get through the hole in the fence, no matter how hard they tried.

Where Is Security?

THE NEXT DAY ALL SIX EGYPTIANS WAITED WITH great impatience for the end of school and the time to meet in the land of Egypt. Everyone was anxious to see if April's question would be answered, but two of the Egyptians had a special reason of their own to be impatient. Marshall had lost his octopus, Security, and there was reason to believe that it had been left in Egypt the night before. Marshall wanted Security back, and Melanie wanted Marshall to quit pestering her and be himself again.

The night before when everyone had left Egypt in such a hurry they had been too busy getting away from the rain—and the darkness and question mysteriously answered—to remember about Security. Not even Marshall had thought of it. And then, just as Marshall and Melanie got back to their apartment, their dad had come in early from the university. He had just been promised a teaching assistantship for the spring semester, and he had been in the mood for a celebration. He had rushed Marshall and Melanie into the car and they had driven to the school where their mom taught, and then they had all gone out to dinner. It was an exciting and unusual evening because until Dad got out of school, money was scarce, and they didn't eat out very often. In fact, it had been such an interesting evening that Marshall hadn't had time to remember about Security until they were home.

Melanie had been climbing into bed when Marshall came into her room. The minute she had looked at him she had known what was wrong—either Security was lost, or the world was coming to an end. It had to be that serious!

Of course, Marshall had wanted to go out right then to Egypt, and Melanie had had a hard time convincing him that it was impossible. It was late, they were both ready for bed, and outdoors the rain was coming down in a great wet roar. Mom and Dad would never let them go alone, and if Dad went with them, the other Egyptians would never forgive them for giving away Egypt to a grown-up. Melanie had known that Marshall understood the importance of what she was saying and that he was trying awfully hard to believe that it was all more important than finding Security. He had gone to the window and stood looking out at the waves of rain that swooshed against the pane. When he came back to Melanie's bed his chin was wiggling. "But—but Security will drown if I don't go get him," he had said.

Melanie had taken hold of his shoulders. "Marshall honey, octopuses can't drown. They live in water," she had said.

Marshall had hung his head. And finally he had sighed and said very softly, "But Security is another kind of octopus."

Just then Melanie had thought of something that helped. "You know what? I'll bet you didn't leave Security in Egypt at all. Now that I think about it, I don't remember seeing him there today. I'll bet you left him at nursery school. I'll bet he's safe and sound in the playroom at nursery school, and you can get him in the morning when you get to school."

Then Melanie had taken Marshall back to his bed and tucked him in. She wasn't at all sure that she believed Security was at the nursery school, and she knew that Marshall didn't either. But they had both tried to believe it as hard as they could.

In the morning it had still been pouring down rain when it was time to go to school, and Melanie's dad had insisted on taking everyone to school in his car on his way to the university—so there had been no chance to check to see if Security really was in the land of Egypt. And, just as they both had feared, he had not been at the nursery school. So there had been nothing they could do but wait for school to be over and the time for Egypt to come.

Fortunately, it had stopped raining during the day, although the sun never came out. But when the time finally came, and all six Egyptians squeezed back through the fence into Egypt—Security wasn't there, either. The storage yard was wet and muddy—and *bare*. Inside the temple, things were damp and messy from the wind-blown rain. Ashes and papers were blown around and some plastic flowers had fallen off the birdbath—but there was no sign of Security anywhere.

That day Marshall wouldn't even take part in the ceremony. He just sat on a box against the fence and watched with big sad eyes. Everybody tried to talk to him and cheer him up, but he wouldn't answer. Looking at him, the others remembered with a feeling of shock that he was awfully little. He usually seemed bigger.

Somehow, no one felt very enthusiastic about starting the ceremony, without really knowing why. It was almost as if they were a little bit afraid of finding out whether there was any mysterious writing on the slip of paper that still hung, damply limp, from Thoth's beak. But at last Melanie, whose turn it was to be high priestess, got things going. She did pretty much what April had done the day before until she got to the part where she took the slip of paper out of Thoth's beak and read it. On one side was April's question, just what Melanie had thought it would be:

When will I go home again?

And on the other side—

Melanie looked up at the other Egyptians with wide eyes, and then she turned and looked, long and hard, at Thoth. Finally she walked right out of the temple, threw the paper on the ground, and said, "I think we just better stop playing this awful game."

Everyone crowded around, grabbing for the paper and asking questions. As it went the rounds, it left a lot of startled faces behind it. The back of the paper, which they all knew had been clean and blank when they had left Egypt the night before, was now covered with writing. In the same small wavery hand that had answered Ken's question, the oracle had written:

The best thing we can do is to make wherever we're lost in Look as much like home as we can.

Again, no one had seen the words being written. Again, what they said didn't sound like anything that a kid would make up. Something very strange was going on. As one person the five biggest Egyptians turned and looked at their temple. There on the left was the altar to Set that they had built themselves from nothing but an old egg crate, and on top of it was the made-by-hand statue of Set, looking a little more sunken and slimy than usual from the blowing rain of the night before. On the right was the birdbath altar with the plaster head of Nefertiti, lovely and gracious in spite of the cracks and chips. And at the back was the new altar to Thoth, with its candles and incense still burning in front of an old stuffed owl that Toby had cut his teeth on.

It had only been a game. Of course, it had been a very special one, more serious and important and mysterious than most—and a lot more fun. And there had been times when it had seemed to have a mysterious sort of reality about it. But no one had believed, when you came right down to it, that it was anything more than a game. At least, no one had until today.

"I think Ross is right," Ken said suddenly. "I told you guys before there was something kooky about this whole thing." He grinned at Toby. "How about it, Tobe? You ready to go back to basketball?"

Toby shrugged. "I think you guys are a bunch of chickens," he said. "Just when things get good and something really exciting starts happening, you want to cop out. What I want to know is, if you don't like a little excitement, why'd you start fooling around with stuff like Egyptian gods and ancient magic in the first place?"

"Look, wise guy," April said, "it just so happens that *I* didn't say I wanted to cop out. And if you're so crazy about excitement why don't you go jump off the bridge or something? That ought to be exciting enough to suit you. It just so happens that some people think there's such a thing as too much excitement."

Toby grinned at April in a way that said he wasn't looking for a fight. "I'm not arguing," he said. "If everyone wants to split, it's all right by me. Let's just forget—"

"No!" Marshall said suddenly in a loud clear voice. It was the first thing he'd said since he found out that Security definitely wasn't in Egypt. "No!" Marshall got up off his box and came over to where the rest of them were standing. His chin was up and he was looking much more like himself. "Let's not stop. Let's not stop till *I* ask a question. I'm going to ask about Security."

Everybody tried to talk him out of it. April and Melanie and Elizabeth all tried because they could see how hard he was going to take it if the oracle didn't come through. And for some reason, Toby tried hardest of all. He squatted down by Marshall and talked to him a long time about how he didn't think that was the kind of question that oracles answered, but Marshall only shut his eyes and shook his head and said "NO!" And everybody knew that Marshall never said *no* unless he meant it.

So Melanie wrote,

WHERE IS SECURITY?

on a piece of paper, because Marshall didn't do much writing yet, and Toby went through the ceremony just as he had the two times before.

Marshall went home acting almost as if Security had already been found, but everyone else went home worried. Melanie and April and Elizabeth and Ken didn't quite know whether to worry because the question might be answered or because it might not be. The whole thing was getting to be so weird and creepy that they couldn't really wish for another answer—but at the same time, what were they going to do about Marshall?

But Toby was the most worried of all.

Confession and Confusion

THAT NIGHT, WHILE THE ORACLE OF THOTH IN THE Land of Egypt struggled with the question "Where is Security?", Toby Alvillar struggled with his conscience. He thought and worried and thought; and at last he broke down and did something entirely against his principles—he called up a girl. When April answered, all he said was, "Look, I got to talk to you and Ross tomorrow early. Meet you out by the parallel bars first recess. Can't talk now—party line."

He had it all worked out so it wouldn't look fishy. When recess started, he went whooping down the hall and down the stairs with the rest of the guys who were headed for the basketball court, but on the way down the stairs he pretended to stumble and turn his ankle. He denied that he was badly hurt, but he managed to look bravely-in-pain as he stumbled over to sit out the recess on the bench near the parallel bars. The girls were in the midst of a jump-rope fad, so the parallel bars were pretty much deserted.

When April and Melanie wandered over—and registered exaggerated surprise to find him there—he got right to the point. "Look," he said, "I was the one who wrote those answers. I was the oracle. But I don't know where Marshall's old octopus is. What're we going to do?"

Of course April and Melanie had a lot to say. They made Toby explain how he'd managed to steal a peek at the questions while he was conducting the ceremonies—while everybody was bowing—and then how he'd looked up the main words in a big book of his dad's, called *Somebody's Famous Quotations*. Then, when he'd picked out a nice mysterious quotation, he'd sneaked back to Egypt at night with a flashlight and written it on the back of the paper.

"But how'd you get out of the house like that, late at night and in the rain and everything? Did your dad know?"

"Did my dad know?" Toby said. Girls could ask the dumbest questions at times. "Fat chance! He never bothers me in the evenings. He's usually working late in the studio or off at an art show somewheres. It was a cinch."

"Weren't you scared?" Melanie asked. "Going down there all by yourself alone in the dark?"

"Well," Toby admitted, "I wasn't exactly whistling 'Yankee Doodle,' if you know what I mean. Did you happen to notice that the oracle's handwriting was a little bit shaky? Well, I didn't just do that to disguise my writing. As a matter of fact, I was about to quit the oracle business even before the rest of you decided to, yesterday. That last night when I went down there, there was somebody in the alley when I was going home."

The girls gasped. "Honestly? In the rain and everything? Are you sure?"

"As sure as I'd want to be. In fact, for a couple of seconds he was just a few steps behind me. It was too dark to see his face—but he was there, all right."

"Ohhh! What did you do? How'd you get away?"

"How'd I get away? Look, Melanie, you ought to know how I got away. Who's been the fastest runner in our class ever since second grade?"

"You," Melanie agreed.

"Right! And when I saw someone behind me, I *really* cut out. I mean—jet-propelled or something."

Toby could always manage to be funny, even about something that was really pretty scary. But after a while, Melanie quit laughing and said, "But who do you think it was? What if it was the man who—"

"The murderer, you mean?" Toby interrupted. "Yeah, I thought of that; all right. Did I ever! But after I got home and calmed down I decided it was probably just some guy taking a shortcut home through the alley. I'm not sure he tried to catch me. I didn't wait around to find out."

The girls laughed some more, but then April sobered up enough to mention that Toby's crimes weren't going entirely unnoticed—fooling everybody, and lying about the oracle—

"Lie to you!" Toby said. "I did not. I didn't lie once. I just gave the wrong impression. There's a difference. Besides, I should think you'd be grateful to me for going to all that trouble just to keep things livened up. My dad says that livening things up is my most outstanding talent. But what I think is, somebody has to do it. Or else everything would just lie there and turn to dust."

"Okay," Melanie said. "So you really livened up the oracle. You livened it up so much that Marshall thinks it's going to tell him where Security is. What are you going to do about *that*?"

"What am *I* going to do about that?" Toby said indignantly. "That's what I got you out here to ask you. What are *we* going to do about Marshall?"

"Well," April and Melanie said to each other—only just with a look, not out loud, "wasn't that like a boy. They got things into a mess and then expected a girl to get them out of it."

But, since Toby was admitting he needed their

help, they were willing to give it. And it didn't take them long to decide on a plan. April would conduct the ceremony that afternoon, and she would pretend to read something off the back of the paper. It would say that Security had gone on a trip to visit his relatives in Los Angeles, and that he would be home in a few days. Marshall wouldn't be completely happy about it, but at least it would give them a little more time to look for Security, or to think of something else.

"Then," Melanie explained, "if we never can find him, at least Marshall will have a few days to get used to the idea, a little at a time. When you lose something like Security, it helps if you can do it sort of gradually." And Toby and April agreed that that was probably true.

Marshall was eager and happy when they picked him up at nursery school. Apparently, he was absolutely positive that the oracle was going to find his octopus for him.

In Egypt, April got ready to be the high priestess again because she had practiced just what she was going to say. Fortunately, there wasn't much chance of an argument. When it came to conducting ceremonies, Ken and Elizabeth were definitely the spectator type.

Everything was going smoothly until April took

down the question and with a dramatic flourish got ready to pretend to read. But then, instead of starting in on her speech about Los Angeles, she let her mouth drop open and nothing came out except a strange gulping sound. Toby bounded into the temple and snatched the paper from her hand. Then he looked at April in a strange way and they both walked over to where the rest of the Egyptians were waiting.

On the back of the paper, in a fine, pointy, old-fashioned-looking handwriting, it said:

Look under the throne of Set

Toby read it out loud very slowly and hesitantly, as if he didn't really believe what he was saying; and while everyone else was still standing as if paralyzed, Marshall went into the temple and lifted up the piece of old bedspread that covered the egg-crate altar of Set. He reached inside, felt around for a minute, and then his face lit up with a smile so starry that for just a second the other, wiser Egyptians felt just as pleased with their oracle as he did. But after that they went right back to being incredulous.

April and Melanie looked hard at Toby, but he shook his head so hard his shaggy hair stood out like an umbrella. "No sir!" he said wildly. "I didn't. I did not! I absolutely did not do it!"

The girls looked at each other and nodded in

agreement that Toby was telling the truth. Nobody, not even Toby, was that good an actor.

"Toby didn't do it," Marshall said, hugging a slightly damp octopus to his chest. "Set did it."

"Set did *what*?" April asked, staring at Marshall in consternation.

"Set took Security. I left him right there on the ground, like I thought, and in the nighttime Set took him."

"Sheee—eeesh!" Ken moaned all of a sudden, clapping his fist violently to his forehead. "I knew it! I knew all you guys were going to crack up someday if you didn't quit fooling around with this hocus-pocus stuff."

"Nobody's cracking up," Toby said thoughtfully, "but something pretty fishy is going on around here."

"You're telling me," Ken said. "And if somebody doesn't start telling me what it is, *I* am going to walk right out of here and resign from the whole Egyptian race!"

"I guess we better, huh?" Toby said to April and Melanie. "I mean, tell everybody all about everything?" The girls nodded.

So they went ahead and told the other three all about what Toby had done—and what Toby *hadn't* done—and when they were through, they all stood and looked at the temple that they had made themselves, out of ordinary stuff and their own imaginations, and felt—well, maybe a little like Dr. Frankenstein had when he created the monster. They just stood there looking for a while and wondering and then they all went home.

Fear Strikes

THE NEXT TWO OR THREE DAYS THE EGYPTIANS MET in Egypt as usual, but they didn't play games or consult the oracle. It was damp, drippy weather but with no real rain, and they all just sat around on the floor of the temple in the darkening late afternoons and talked and talked. Toby and April wanted to try the oracle once more to see what would happen, but no one else seemed very enthusiastic. Oh, they said "okay," but somehow it kept getting put off. They talked about it—but that was all.

They talked about a lot of things, actually. Christmas wasn't far away, and that's always a good topic for conversation. But there was one subject they kept coming back to—Security. Where had Security been? How had he gotten from wherever Marshall had left him to the hiding place beneath the altar of Set?

And who had written the message? There were dozens of theories, more or less realistic, depending on the mood of the moment.

There were times when they all favored practical theories. Some other kids might have found out about the game and tried to be funny. But, as time went by, and no one burst in on them to gloat about the successful trick, that seemed less and less likely. Or, someone of their own group might have been guilty, just as Toby had been at first; but no one would confess, and there just didn't seem to be any reasonable how and why to support a conclusion of that sort. Then there was the man Toby had seen in the alley— but no one could come up with an even slightly reasonable explanation of who he was and how he could have known about the oracle.

Of course, the subject of the murders and the murderer came up, as it often still did throughout the neighborhood. It was still an unsolved mystery, and a terribly real and dangerous one. But fortunately, here again, there seemed to be no logical reason to believe that *that* mystery could have any connection with the mystery of the oracle. Why would a murderer fool around writing messages about a missing toy? There seemed to be no possible answer.

At other times, when the afternoon was almost over and disturbing shadows crept across the storage yard, a different kind of theory went the rounds.

Somebody brought up the story of the Curse of King Tut, and pointed out that lots of people actually believed that a mysterious magic power from the days of the pharaohs was strong enough to do terrible things to anyone who stirred it up. What if somehow, in their ceremonies and things, they'd managed to stumble on a way to do some stirring up themselves? Things like that had happened. Everyone had read something or seen something on TV like that. And they all began to remember strange things that had happened. Once when Melanie had touched the Crocodile Stone, she was sure she'd felt it move under her fingers. And another time, when Toby had gotten to Egypt early and alone, he'd had the strangest feeling that someone was watching him.

Once they got going on that sort of thing, they all had stories and experiences to tell. That is, all except Marshall. He just sat, holding Security on his lap and listening, and if he had any theories about mysterious powers or hidden watchers, he kept them strictly to himself.

Then one evening there was to be a concert at the university and the Rosses decided to go. They were planning to take Melanie, but since Marshall had a way of going to sleep at concerts, it seemed best to leave him at home. April had some homework to do anyway, and she agreed to come down and baby-sit until the Rosses got back.

It was around 7:30 when Melanie called to say they were leaving and April said she would be right down. It wasn't until she started to get her things together that she realized her math book was missing. She looked all over the apartment but she couldn't find it anywhere. At last she had to give up and go without it.

When April got to the second floor, the Rosses were waiting for her in the hall. As soon as they saw her, they waved good-bye and got into the elevator. Marshall was standing in the doorway.

"Hello," he said. "They said you were coming to visit." Marshall didn't like people to say "baby-sitter," but he didn't mind having someone "visit" him while his folks were away. So April took some time to make it a real visit before she started her own work. They played a game of Mousetrap, and April read aloud a short book about a hippopotamus. Then Marshall went back to something he was doing with a box and two orange juice cans, and April started her homework.

It was just about then that she finally remembered what had probably happened to her math book. That afternoon, in Egypt, she'd put her books down on the edge of the temple floor and Ken had been fooling around and knocked them off. He'd sort of picked them up when she yelled at him, but he must have left the math book on the ground.

April sat there fuming for a few minutes, getting madder and madder at Ken. It was all his fault. For the first time in her life she had been getting pretty good grades in math, and now her record was going to be ruined—all because of Ken. Mrs. Granger was terribly strict about getting assignments in on time. All of a sudden she jumped up. "Marshall," she called. "Do your folks have a flashlight?"

When Marshall came back with the flashlight, she told him what she had in mind.

"Aren't you scared?" Marshall asked.

Now that he'd mentioned it, April had to admit to herself that she was. But being scared and chickening out were two different things. Being scared to do something had always made April more determined to do it than ever. Besides, if Toby could go down there all alone at night, so could she.

"Me? Scared?" she said. "Don't be ridiculous."

"Wait," Marshall said. He went in the bedroom and came out with his sweater and Security.

"Now, just a minute," April said. "You can't go. I won't let you."

Marshall put his sweater on inside out, all by himself. "Don't be ridiculous," he said.

"Your folks wouldn't like it," April argued. "I'll only be gone a minute. You're going to wait right here."

Marshall was puzzling over his buttons, which

were on the wrong side, and he didn't answer.

"I mean it," April said. "Whether you like it or not, you are only four years old, and *I* am taking care of you and you have to do what I say. And I say that you are going to stay right here and—"

Marshall gave up on the buttons. He picked up Security and walked out the door, into the hallway. He aimed himself down the stairs towards where the landlady lived. "I'll yell," he said.

For a few seconds April stared at him in silence. Then she said some things under her breath and, because there didn't seem to be anything else to do, she took Marshall by the hand and they started out.

It was very quiet and very dark in the alley and familiar things loomed up suddenly, huge and out of shape. The flashlight beam, none too steady in April's hand, made trash bins crouch and garbage pails lurk, and a length of hose slither against a wall. Imagination is a great thing in long dull hours, but it's a real curse in a dark alley, and April's imagination had always been out of the ordinary. She would have hated to admit it, but right at that moment, even a four-year-old was a little bit comforting. Especially a four-year-old who could march steadfastly by a garbage can that had suddenly developed a hunchback and great lopsided eyes, without even seeming to notice.

It was April's imagination that made trouble when

they got to the fence; because if she hadn't been imagining she wouldn't have been so nervous. And if she hadn't been so nervous, she wouldn't have pushed the board the wrong way. All the Egyptians always pushed it to the right, and it no longer squeaked when it swung that way.

But that night, probably because of the nervousness, April grabbed the board and shoved it the wrong way. And the big crooked nails on which it swung let out a wild rusty shriek.

April and Marshall froze into a shocked silence. In the dark quiet alley the shriek of the nails seemed unbelievably loud. It seemed perfectly possible that people a half-block away had heard it and would come running. But a half minute passed, and then perhaps a whole minute, and nobody came and not a sound was heard. At least, not a sound that was loud enough to be sure of. There was something—a faint and far-away click and then a dragging shuffle—so soft as to be almost entirely lost in the distant drone of traffic and the beating of a racing heart.

Finally, biting her lip, April pushed the board the other way and shoved Marshall through. Then she handed him the flashlight and squeezed through herself. Inside Egypt, April didn't feel very much better. Ever since the unsolved mystery of the oracle, Egypt, although still fascinating, had ceased to be an entirely comfortable place. She went directly to the side of the temple where her books had been.

"Marshall," she whispered, "shine the light over here. I can't see a thing." Marshall for some reason had turned around and was aiming the light in the opposite direction, on the wall of the Professor's store, but at her whisper he turned back. The book was right where she thought it would be, shoved partway back under the temple floor. She snatched it up and with a hurried glance at the temple, where the three altars were only blobs of darkest black on a black background, she hurried back to the fence.

As Marshall held the light on the right spot, April reached through, shoved the board to the right side, and squeezed out. She was holding the board open for Marshall when, out of the darkness and silence behind, something grabbed her with crushing strength, and big hard fingers smothered the scream that sprang into her throat.

In one terrible moment April found that the shock of certain danger is almost always a battle call. Twisting frantically, she managed to free her arms enough to reach for and grab the loose board that formed the door to the storage yard. She held on desperately and the nails shrieked again as the board swung far to one side. For a fraction of a second April's eyes, above the hand that gagged her mouth, caught a glimpse of Marshall, still standing just inside the fence holding the flashlight and looking back over his shoulder at the wall behind him. "What's wrong with him?" she thought frantically. "Why doesn't he scream for help?"

The board was slipping slowly from April's straining fingers, and the arm around her chest was forcing the air from her lungs, when suddenly, from inside the storage yard, there was a splintering crash and a strange hoarse shout. "Help!" the strange voice rasped. "Help!"

A window went up with a bang somewhere nearby, and farther away other voices began to call questions. "What? What is it? What's the matter?" And all the while the first strange voice went on calling for help.

Then there were footsteps and shouts at the mouth of the alley and suddenly the crushing arms were gone. When the rescuers arrived a moment later, they found April lying on the ground and Marshall squeezing out to meet them through the fence. No one else was there, and the only sound was the rasp of April's breathing as she struggled to force air back into her lungs.

The Hero

AFTERWARDS, GETTING TO THE POLICE STATION AND the first things that happened there were always hazy in April's mind. There was a doctor who talked to her and bandaged her hands where she had scraped them on the rough board. Then there were questions. She explained how she and Marshall happened to be in the alley, but the other questions she couldn't answer and it frightened her to try. "Who was he?" they kept saying. "What did he look like? Where did he go?" and April could only say, "I don't know. I didn't see him. I don't know. I don't know."

They tried to make her lie down on a cot but she kept wanting to get up because she was shaking so hard. Whenever she tried to lie still, the shaking would get worse and worse until she ached from trying to stop it. Then the doctor gave her a pill, and the shaking got a little better and things were clearer in her mind.

Suddenly she remembered about Marshall. "Where's Marshall?" she asked. "Is he all right?"

The man who had been asking the most questions was called Inspector Grant. He wasn't wearing a uniform, but he was a policeman. When April asked about Marshall, he grinned. "He's fine," he said. "He's right in the next room over there."

"He's really all right," April insisted. "He's not too scared, or anything?"

"Well, he doesn't act a bit scared," the inspector said. "He's sitting in there on a desk holding a big stuffed octopus and looking as cool as a cucumber. But he won't answer any questions."

"Won't he talk to anybody?" April said.

"Oh, he talks to us," Inspector Grant said. "He's been asking us a lot of questions, in fact. He just won't answer any. Every time we ask anything he just says, 'No.' We think he might have seen more than you did. Do you suppose he'd answer a few questions if you ask him?"

"He might," April said. "I don't know."

When Marshall saw April he slid down off the desk and came running. "Hi," he said, giving her one of his rare starry smiles. April hugged him hard. Then she asked what the inspector had told her to ask.

"Marshall, did you see the—the man—the man who grabbed me?" Saying the words made the shaking start all over again.

"Yes," Marshall said. "I saw him. I tried to yell but I couldn't. My throat was stuck." He looked worried, as if he wanted to be sure that April understood.

"You did fine," April told him. "But about the man —what did he look like?"

"A man. A big man."

"Was he young or old?"

Marshall thought a minute. "Old," he said.

"What color was his hair?"

"Orange."

April looked at Inspector Grant. "Ask about his race," the policeman prompted.

"Was he a black or a white man?" April asked.

"No," Marshall said thoughtfully, shaking his head.

April thought he didn't understand. She took his arm and rubbed her finger on his skin. "Was his skin like yours or like mine?" She held out her own arm.

"No," Marshall said, more firmly. "He was spotted."

"Would you know him if you saw him again?" Inspector Grant interrupted.

Marshall only looked at him without answering. The inspector gave an exasperated sigh and turned to

April. "He's not just being stubborn," April explained. "I think he just wants to be sure he isn't telling a secret. Marshall never tells secrets." She turned to Marshall and repeated the question.

Marshall nodded. "Yes. I know him." Just then there was a commotion at the door and Inspector Grant stood up. April wasn't sure if he heard Marshall say, "He's that man who carries things at the store."

The inspector hurried to the door and April heard him say, "The boy says he'd know the man if he saw him." There was more talk and confusion and finally a man was led into the room. It was the Professor.

April was sure it was the Professor, but he looked quite different from her memory of him. His hair was mussed, his face moved nervously, and the dead calm was gone from his eyes. He looked at Marshall, and Marshall looked at him. "Hello," Marshall said.

The inspector took hold of April's arm and whispered a question. She gazed at the Professor in horror. Could it have been? Had he really been the one all the time? All that time while they were playing every day in his yard. Obediently, but with a shaky voice, she transferred the question to Marshall.

"Marshall, is that the man? Is that the one who grabbed me?"

"No," Marshall said. "That's the man who watches us all the time. He was looking out his window, like always. He was the one who said, 'Help.'"

The Professor smiled wearily. "That's what I've been trying to tell you—"

But now Marshall realized that they still hadn't understood. He shook April's arm to get her attention and explained it all again as patiently as he could. "I told you!" he said. "I told you who it was. It was that spotted man with orange hair. The one who carries things at the toy store."

At last April understood. "Oh-h-h," she said. "I think he means that redheaded man who works for Mr. Schmitt sometimes. He's a stockboy or something."

Two of the policemen hurried off, and Inspector Grant led April back to the other room and told her to lie down again and rest. This time Marshall came with them and climbed up on a chair beside the cot. He put Security on his lap and looked around with interest. Seeing him there made April feel calmer.

She lay on the cot and tried to keep from shivering. And she tried not to think about the redheaded man. Instead she thought about the Professor. "Marshall," she said, raising up on one elbow, "did you say the Professor's been watching us?"

Marshall nodded. "Out his window," he said. "And he broke it with a stick and said, 'Help.' I couldn't. My throat was stuck."

It gave April a funny feeling to think that they'd been watched all that time, or at least whenever the Professor felt like it—but it was certainly a good thing he'd been watching tonight. It was a good thing he "said help," as Marshall put it.

The inspector, who was sitting at the other end of the cot, broke in as if he could read her thoughts. "It was certainly lucky that the old man was there to shout for help," he said. "You know that's the best thing to do in a situation like that. Your voice is your best defense."

"But I couldn't call," April said, covering her face and trying not to remember so vividly the fingers across her mouth and throat. Inspector Grant leaned over and patted her shoulder.

"I know," he said soothingly. "But it's all over now. And it all worked out just fine, didn't it. You're all right, and Marshall here has been a real detective."

"Why did they think the Professor did it?" April asked after a while.

"Well, they weren't sure, of course," the inspector said. "But some of the officers thought he was a pretty good suspect. Living right there in the neighborhood, and he couldn't give us an alibi for the nights when the other—for the other times. And then tonight, with it happening right in his backyard and all. And when some of the boys went to the door of his store and he came running out looking wild-eyed and excited, it seemed best to bring him in for questioning at least. He told them that he'd called for help from his window, but I guess they weren't buying his story much, until Marshall stood up for him."

It was then that Caroline came in. She ran across the room and hugged April up into her arms and held her tight. When April realized that Caroline was crying, she began to cry, too. She hadn't cried at all until then, and she really didn't want to, but when they both stopped crying, the tension was gone and the shaking, and she felt much better. She was suddenly very tired and sleepy. "Grandma," she said, "would you ask them if we can go home now? I'm terribly tired."

To Marshall's delight they rode home in a police car, and they left a note on the Rosses' door because they weren't back from the concert yet. It was amazing to April to think that so little time had passed—it seemed like years and years. In their own apartment they made a bed for Marshall on the couch and he went right off to sleep as if nothing had happened, with his arm around Security. April went to bed, too, but it took her a long time to get to sleep, and Caroline sat beside the bed until she finally did. April always hated to be fussed over, but it *was* sort of nice to open her eyes now and then and see Caroline just sitting there, quietly reading a book.

Of course, the math didn't get done; but as it turned out, it didn't really matter, because April stayed home from school the next day, and her grandmother took the day off, too. April was feeling fine, except for the bandages on her hands and some bruises on her cheeks and ribs. In the afternoon the police came to take her back to the station to look at some men in the lineup. She wasn't much help because she really hadn't seen the man at all. But Marshall had to go, and he wanted April to come, too, and the police seemed to think that she might remember something that would be useful.

When the men came in for the lineup, there was the big stocky man with red hair and blotchy red-brown freckles from Schmitt's Variety Store, the one who was the stockboy, and Marshall pointed to him right away. April remembered that when she had seen him in the store, he had seemed quiet and shy, and in the lineup he looked bewildered, as if he didn't understand what had happened.

The next day it was all in the papers. The red-headed man had admitted everything. There wasn't going to be a real trial because the man was very sick mentally and was to be sent to a hospital for the criminally insane. He was a relative of Mr. Schmitt and he had always had something wrong with his mind. He couldn't get a good job, and sometimes Mr. Schmitt let him work as a stockboy in his store. He'd work for a while and then he'd go away and do something else. But he always came back again, and since he was willing to work for very little money, Mr. Schmitt always hired him again. The police hadn't found out about him before because Mr. Schmitt had always given him an alibi. But when the redheaded man confessed, and told all about things he couldn't have known unless he was guilty, Mr. Schmitt decided that he hadn't been positive of his cousin's whereabouts at the times of the crimes. He only thought he knew.

April's picture was in the paper and so was Marshall's. There was a long story about how Marshall had saved the Professor from being unjustly accused and described the murderer so that the police were able to catch him. But April and Melanie were a little bit disgusted with the way the reporter talked about Marshall's description. After all, he was spotted, in a way, and his hair was more orange than anything else. He really wasn't old, as Marshall had said; but, as Melanie pointed out, when you are only four yourself, almost anybody's old by comparison.

Anyway, Marshall was a real hero around the neighborhood. Everyone wanted to see him and ask him questions about what happened. The Rosses tried to keep him home for a while because they said they didn't want him getting an exaggerated notion of his own importance. But they needn't have worried. Marshall took the whole thing very calmly. In fact, being a hero didn't seem to change him a bit except for one thing.

When the photographer came to take his picture for the paper, Marshall took Security into the bedroom and put him on his bed. He said Security didn't want his picture taken. After that he started leaving

Security home sometimes when he went places, and before too long he didn't need to have Security with him at all anymore, excepting to hold on to at night when he was sleepy.

Gains and Losses

THINGS HAD SCARCELY HAD TIME TO QUIET DOWN after April's narrow escape when Christmas vacation arrived. The first few days of vacation, the members of the Egypt gang were pretty busy with family things like shopping and trips and relatives, but now and then some of their paths crossed and they stopped to discuss things in general, and the Egypt situation in particular. That situation didn't look good at all.

The day after all the excitement, Toby had drifted down the alley just to look things over, and he had found the land of Egypt boarded up. Someone had replaced the loose board and nailed it into place with big, long nails, and some fresh strands of barbed wire had been strung around the top. The consensus of opinion was pretty much, "That's that!" Egypt was lost and gone forever, and there was no use thinking about it. It was a terrible loss.

As a matter of fact, the Egyptians hadn't really realized until then just how great Egypt had been. It had been a terrific game, full of excitement and mystery and way-out imagining, but it had been a great deal more than that. It had been a place to get away to—a private lair—a secret seclusion meant to be shared with best friends only—a life unknown to grown-ups and lived by kids alone. And now, all of a sudden, it was gone.

But the other Egyptians didn't blame April and Marshall for its loss. After all, they hadn't done it on purpose, and the way it turned out they had really done all the kids in the neighborhood a big favor—because now that the murderer had been caught everybody was being allowed a lot more freedom. The whole neighborhood had benefited, really. There was only Egypt to mourn.

It was a few days after the beginning of vacation that April decided to go down and pay a visit to the Professor, or Dr. Huddleston, as people were beginning to call him. The visit had been her grandmother's suggestion in the first place, but April agreed that it was a good idea. As she started downstairs, she considered stopping by for Melanie, but she decided against it. It was better to go alone on such a personal errand. And she really did have something very personal to say.

But if April had imagined that it would be easy to

have a quiet personal interview with the Professor in his lonely store, she was mistaken. There were two or three browsers just looking around; the Professor was wrapping something up for a customer; and over by the window Elizabeth's mother, Mrs. Chung, was dusting some figurines and arranging them in the display case. The whole store looked different—cleaner and brighter and not so cluttered. April was amazed.

For one thing, Mrs. Chung had been working at a cleaners over on the other side of town, and April hadn't heard anything about a change. But then, Elizabeth had been visiting in San Francisco with her cousins the last few days, so April wasn't really up to date on the Chung family news.

"Hi, Mrs. Chung," April said. "Do you work here now?"

"Hello, April. Yes I do. I just began on Monday."

It didn't look as if the Professor was going to be free very soon, so April squatted down to look at the tiny foreign-looking statues that Mrs. Chung was arranging very artistically on a velvet cloth.

"I think this would be a neat place to work," April said. "I'd sure like it."

"It's a very interesting place to work," Mrs. Chung said. "And it's wonderful being so close to home. I think I'm going to like it very much. Dr. Huddleston is planning to do some traveling soon to look for new things to sell, and I'll be in charge here while he's gone." Mrs. Chung smiled delightedly, and April noted that her dimples were just like Elizabeth's.

"There sure are a lot of people in here," April mentioned, just to make conversation.

Mrs. Chung smiled. "I guess it's been that way all the time lately. Poor Dr. Huddleston's almost worn himself out taking care of them. Of course, some of them are just curious, because of all the publicity and everything in the papers. But a lot of them are neighborhood people who are feeling ashamed about suspecting him when he was innocent. They come in here and buy things they don't even need, just to ease their consciences."

April grinned. "I'll bet the people who signed that petition Mr. Schmitt sent around buy the most of all."

"No doubt," Mrs. Chung said. "I've heard that Mr. Schmitt is selling out. This whole thing must have been very hard on him."

"Well, I don't feel sorry for him," April said. "I'll bet he had a notion that his cousin was the murderer but he didn't want to believe it. And that was why he was so sure it was the Professor. That's what my grandmother says."

"I guess that's something we'll never know," Mrs. Chung said. She nodded towards the Professor. "I think Dr. Huddleston is free now if you wanted to see him."

The Professor shook April's hand, and he smiled

ever so slightly when she said, "I came to say thanks a lot for saving my life." He looked pretty much as April remembered him and his voice was still gravelly and grave, but he seemed younger, somehow, and more lively.

"You're most welcome," he said. "But I'm not at all sure I was responsible. I feel sure your young friend would have found some other means to aid you if I had not been available."

"Oh, you mean Marshall?" April said. "Yeah, isn't he something!"

The Professor agreed that he certainly was, and then there was an uncomfortable pause and April for once was at a loss for words.

At last the Professor said, "I have something here you might like to see." He took down a small box and opened it carefully on the counter. There were two objects in it, a flat piece of marble with dim hieroglyphics on it, and a small head of a glowing milky white.

"Ohhh," April said. "That's alabaster, isn't it?"

"Very good," the Professor said. "You're quite an Egyptologist. And the other is a bit of marble facing from the wall of a tomb."

They examined the pieces together, and the Professor told April all sorts of interesting things about them. He also said that they had once belonged to his wife—and that was an interesting idea in itself, to think that the lonely old Professor had once had a wife. In the course of the conversation it occurred to April that this would be a good time to mention all the things that had been left in the land of Egypt. The six Egyptians had thought about them many times and wondered if the Professor intended to give them back. Toby, in particular, hated to lose Thoth— he was a sort of keepsake. Two or three times she was on the verge of mentioning it, but each time she lost her nerve. After all, they had put the things on the Professor's property, and maybe that meant they were his now. And you just can't go around demanding things of someone who's just saved your life.

But, except for the fact that the Professor didn't offer to give back their things, it was a very successful visit. As April was getting ready to go, she said, "Well, good-bye, and thanks again, Profes—I mean Dr. Huddleston. My grandmother says your name is Dr. Julian Huddleston. Are you really a doctor?"

"Not a medical doctor. A doctor of philosophy—a Ph.D. I once taught at the university, but that was a long time ago. I'd be most pleased if you and your friends continued to call me the Professor. I'd prefer it, in fact."

"So do I," April said. "Okay, good-bye, Professor. And thanks again."

When April got back to the apartment, there was a letter waiting for her. It was from her mother. It was

the first letter April had had for over a month. Of
course, Dorothea would probably have written if she'd
known about April's narrow escape, but she hadn't
known. For some reason, April hadn't told her, and
she'd asked Caroline not to either. When Caroline
had asked April why, she'd just said, "I don't know.
What's the use. It's too late now."

But today there was a letter, and an invitation.

> Darling,
>
> Nick and I are planning on spending
> three or four days in Palm Springs over
> Christmas. We want you to hop on a
> plane and fly down to us. There'll be
> swimming and sunning and lots of fun.
> We'll meet you at the airport if you let
> us know when and where. We're dying
> to see you again.
>
> Love,
> Dorothea

April took the letter to her room. She sat down by
the window and reread it three times and felt around
inside herself for reactions. She found some, all right,
both good and bad; but not nearly as much either
way as she would have expected. Not as much happi-
ness to be asked, and not nearly as much anger to be
asked so late and for so little. After a while she got out

some paper and wrote an answer. Then she took both letters and went looking for Caroline. She found her in the kitchen sewing sequins on a Christmas stocking made of felt. Without saying anything, April put the letters down in front of her.

> Dear Dorothea, (*April's letter said*)
> Thank you for inviting me to Palm Springs. It sounds like lots of fun. But Grandma and I have our plans all made for Christmas Eve and I have a date to spend part of Christmas Day with my friend, Melanie. So I guess I can't make it this time.
>
> > Love,
> > April
>
> P.S. You should see our tree. We decorated it yesterday and it's great.

Caroline was such a quiet person it was hard sometimes to know what she was thinking. But lately, April usually thought she could tell. Right then, Caroline only smiled and said, "That's a very nice letter, dear," and bent her head back down over the sequins. And the sun coming in the little stained-glass section of the breakfast room window made her smooth gray hair look just like a pigeon's wing.

Christmas Keys

On the morning of Christmas Eve, Caroline had a telephone call from the Professor, and afterwards she asked April to phone all the members of the Egypt gang and ask them to come to the Halls' for just a few minutes that night after dinner. "The Professor wants to see you," she said. "He said he knows you'll all want to be with your families tonight and he won't keep you long. But he wants to see all six of you for just a few minutes."

"What for?" April asked.

"I think he wants it to be a surprise," Caroline said.

So April called up all the other Egyptians and made the invitation sound just as mysterious and intriguing as she could. Personally, she had a suspicion that the Professor was just going to give back all their stuff, but as Toby said, there's nothing like keeping things livened up.

After dinner Caroline made some hot spiced cider, and April arranged a plate of fancy Christmas cookies that she and Caroline had baked. Just about then the guests started to arrive. Ken and Toby came first, looking slightly embarrassed to be visiting where a girl lived. Then Melanie arrived with Marshall, and Elizabeth came a few minutes afterwards. They sat around for a while drinking cider and listening to a Christmas carol program. They speculated about what the Professor had in mind, and had just about agreed that he was probably bringing back all their stuff, when he arrived—apparently empty-handed. So that was the end of that theory.

The Professor gave April his coat and said hello to everyone in his strange formal way. Caroline got everyone seated again and turned the music down very low; but for a while they all just sat there feeling uncomfortable. The whole situation was so unusual that nobody knew quite how to act.

At last the Professor put down his cup, looked around the room, and said, "I've come to tell you a story."

Out of the corner of her eye, April saw Ken and Toby exchange raised eyebrows. She narrowed her eyes and nailed them both with her fiercest glare.

When somebody saves your life, it makes him sort of your property, and nobody was going to make fun of the Professor with April around, even if he was going to treat them as if they were little kids.

"A Christmas story?" Marshall asked.

"No—" the Professor began, but then he paused. "Yes," he said, "I suppose it is. I suppose it is a Christmas story, in a way. But it's a sad story—a terrible story—too terrible for children, perhaps. And yet, I feel that it's something the six of you ought to know."

April felt, rather than saw, Ken and Toby prick up their ears. She gave an internal nod of approval. He had them now. The Professor was doing all right.

"The story begins when I was a young man. I was really a professor then, at the university. I was always a very quiet and reserved person and at that time my life, even my work, was beginning to seem rather dull and routine. But then one day, a young woman enrolled in one of my classes and changed my entire way of life. Her name was Anne."

April and Melanie looked at each other and their eyes made extravagant comments.

"Anne was an artist," the Professor went on. "My subject was anthropology, which, as you may know, is the study of all the various kinds and conditions of mankind. Anne was not particularly interested in anthropology, but she enrolled in a class I was teaching on primitive and ancient peoples because of her interest in primitive art. Anne used to tease me about anthropology—she said anthropologists were only interested in people in general and she liked people in particular—and she did, too. All kinds of people. She was at ease with everyone—lighthearted, fun-loving, enthusiastic and optimistic. There was a hopefulness about her— Well, after we were married I began to see life in a new way.

"Anne was delighted when I decided to travel and do research. While I studied various tribes, she studied their art forms and collected samples of their crafts. And usually she managed to get involved in various efforts to improve the living conditions of the people of the area. The A–Z store was Anne's idea, in the beginning. Her plan was to make it an outlet for some of the native handicrafts from areas where we had worked. It was on our last visit home together that she bought the building and made the first arrangements."

The Professor paused as if he was trying to think what to say next. "On our last trip," he went on at last, "Anne was visiting a mission where she was trying to set up a production center for native handicrafts. The people of the area were very poor and she thought it would provide them with a means of earning a better living. There had been some unrest in the next province, but we thought— Well, there was an uprising, a small local rebellion. The mission was attacked and Anne was killed—by the very people she was trying to help.

"I came back here. I had no desire to teach, so I sold our house and moved into Anne's store. I had some idea of opening the store and operating it along the lines that Anne had planned, but I soon gave it up. I gradually broke off many of the contacts that Anne had made and let the store become a junk shop. I had a small income so I didn't have to make the business pay, but for some reason I kept the store open.

"As the years went by, the store and I became dusty junkyards, and after a while I didn't care."

The Professor looked up and around the circle of intent faces, and his lips moved in their slight smile. "And then one day," he said, "I heard a strange noise in my storage yard. At first, I told myself I was watching to make sure nothing was damaged and no fires were started. You know, sacred fires can be just as dangerous as ordinary ones. Then, after the murder, when my business dropped to almost nothing and I had little else to do, I watched more and more often."

"You mean, you watched us do the Ceremony for the Dead and the oracle and all that stuff?" April asked.

"Yes, all of that."

The Egyptians exchanged sheepish glances, and Ken hit himself on the forehead in an agony of embarrassment. "Sheesh!" he moaned.

"The oracle!" Toby said suddenly. "Hey! You didn't have anything to do with—"

The Professor nodded. "I'm afraid I must plead guilty to that, too. I watched you leave that night and I saw the octopus left behind in the rain. I went out and pried open the old padlock and went into the yard. The wind was blowing the rain into the shed quite badly and under the altar covering seemed the driest place. I was getting wet and was in such a hurry that I didn't stop to consider that it might be hard to find. Then, as I was watching the next day I suddenly conceived of a plan to direct you to the lost article by way of"—he paused and his lips moved again in his small stiff smile—"the oracle.

"What I did then, in behalf of Security, was done on the spur of the moment, and afterwards I tried not to think about it. I think I decided to play the part of the oracle because I felt obligated to let you know what I had done with Security, and the oracle offered a way to do it without any direct contact. And contact —involvement—was what I had spent years eliminating entirely from my life.

"I had begun to suspect, however, that one of you" —the Professor looked at Marshall—"knew that I was watching. But he was very careful in the way he watched back. I wasn't entirely sure until the night of the attempt on April's life.

"I was reading when I heard a sound in the storage yard and, of course, I went immediately to the window. When I saw—when I realized what was happening, my first reaction was the natural one. I grabbed up a block of wood—but then, twenty-five years of self-imprisonment took control. I couldn't bring myself to break the glass and call.

"I stood there holding the block of wood in my hand, and then Marshall turned around and looked at me. I could see that he knew that I was there and that he was asking me ·to help. And then I broke the glass—"

The Professor's voice stopped and everyone waited until, at last, it became clear that his story was over, even though it hadn't sounded like an ending at all. For a long time no one moved or talked. The room was very still except for a boys' choir singing "Hark the Herald Angels" very softly on the radio.

But then Marshall leaned over and poked Melanie. "Is *that* the end?" he whispered loudly.

"Shhh!" Melanie said, and nodded.

"But what was the Christmas part?" Marshall whispered even more loudly.

The Professor must have heard Marshall but he didn't answer. Instead he began to feel around in his jacket pocket. There was a jingling sound, and he brought out a handful of shiny new keys. The keys had long chains to wear around your neck, and on the head part of each one a name was engraved. The Professor read off the names one by one and handed out the keys. "Elizabeth, Toby, Melanie—"

"Is it—is it to Egypt?" Elizabeth whispered as she took her key, and at the Professor's nod there was a storm of comment.

"Hey, neat!"

"Awesome!"

"Thanks a lot."

"Hey, yeah, thanks."

"Thanks a lot."

"Of course, you'll have to enter on the other side of the yard now," the Professor said. "I've had a new padlock put on the door—a padlock with just six keys—"

Caroline got up and went to the kitchen for a fresh round of cider and cookies, but everyone was too busy talking and planning to be much interested in food. "No, not tomorrow," Melanie said. "Tomorrow's Christmas and we'll have to be home most of the time. But the next day—"

"Yeah," Toby agreed, "we'll be doing the togetherness bit at our pad tomorrow, too. My dad's even promised to stay out of his studio all day. But the day after's okay by me."

So the date was made—Egypt, the day after Christmas, right after lunch. Then everybody got up and started getting ready to go home. At the door Ken turned back. "Uh, Professor," he said. "Are you going to—that is—are you still going to watch us all the time?"

Everybody laughed. "No, I'm afraid I won't have time," the Professor said. "I seem to have gotten myself involved in being a real storekeeper. I'm going to try to do some importing again, handicrafts and curios. I'll be doing quite a bit of traveling for a while until I get my stock lined up. But perhaps, once in a while when I'm home, you'll invite me to a special occasion."

"Sure," Toby said, "that'll be great. And thanks again for the great present. I sure wish we had something for you."

"Yes," some of the others chimed in. "We should have brought something for you."

The Professor held up his hand. "But I thought you understood," he said. "You've already made me a gift—a very important one." He smiled his strange solemn smile and put his hand on Marshall's head. "That's how I should have ended my story—if I could have explained it—with your gift to me. That would have been the Christmas part. That's what makes it a Christmas story."

Late the next afternoon April and Melanie lay across April's bed and chatted. They were stuffed to contented laziness with Christmas dinner and they had been down to Melanie's apartment to look at her presents and then up to look at April's.

They had talked about Christmas and presents until the subject was exhausted and then they began to talk about the keys and the Professor and what he'd said the evening before.

They just lay there for a while, dreaming and digesting, and then Melanie suddenly sat up. "I feel sad," she said.

April made a "why?" expression. "Oh, I don't know," Melanie said. "It's about Egypt. Going back and everything. It seems like it won't be the same."

"Yeah," April said. "I thought about that, too."

"We'll go back, thinking it will be so terrific—and what will we do? The same things all over again? We've done just about everything exciting about Egypt."

"Yeah, and it's just awful when you go back to

something that was so great the way you remembered it and it's no good anymore. It even ruins remembering."

Melanie nodded tragically and they both collapsed again. They lay there, staring into the future gloomily for a while, their chins on their hands. Then April turned towards Melanie, slowly and thoughtfully.

"Melanie," she said, "what do you know about Gypsies?"

Turn the page for a special preview
of the

1996 NEWBERY HONOR BOOK

(ISBN 0-385-32175-9)

Enter the hilarious world of ten-year-old Kenny and his
family, the Weird Watsons of Flint, Michigan. There's
Momma, Dad, little sister Joetta, Kenny, and Byron, who's
thirteen and an "official juvenile delinquent." When Momma
and Dad decide it's time for a visit to Grandma, Dad comes
home with the amazing Ultra-Glide, and the Watsons set out
on a trip like no other. They're heading south. They're going
to Birmingham, Alabama, toward one of the darkest
moments in American history.

**Don't miss *The Watsons Go to Birmingham–1963*
by Christopher Paul Curtis.
On sale now from Delacorte Press!**

1. And You Wonder Why We Get Called the Weird Watsons

It was one of those super-duper-cold Saturdays. One of those days that when you breathed out your breath kind of hung frozen in the air like a hunk of smoke and you could walk along and look exactly like a train blowing out big, fat, white puffs of smoke.

It was so cold that if you were stupid enough to go outside your eyes would automatically blink a thousand times all by themselves, probably so the juice inside of them wouldn't freeze up. It was so cold that if you spit, the slob would be an ice cube before it hit the ground. It was about a zillion degrees below zero.

It was even cold inside our house. We put sweaters and hats and scarves and three pairs of socks on and still were cold. The thermostat was turned all the way up and the furnace was banging and sounding like it was about to blow up but it still felt like Jack Frost had moved in with us.

All of my family sat real close together on the couch under a blanket. Dad said this would generate a little heat but he didn't have to tell us this, it seemed like the cold automatically made us want to get together and huddle up. My little sister, Joetta, sat in the middle and all you could see were her eyes because she had a scarf wrapped around her head. I was next to her, and on the outside was my mother.

Momma was the only one who wasn't born in Flint so the cold was coldest to her. All you could see were her eyes too, and they were shooting bad looks at Dad. She always blamed him for bringing her all the way from Alabama to Michigan, a state she called a giant icebox. Dad was bundled up on the other side of Joey, trying to look at anything but Momma. Next to Dad, sitting with a little space between them, was my older brother, Byron.

Byron had just turned thirteen so he was officially a teenage juvenile delinquent and didn't think it was "cool" to touch anybody or let anyone touch him, even if it meant he froze to death. Byron had tucked the blanket between him and Dad down into the cushion of the couch to make sure he couldn't be touched.

Dad turned on the TV to try to make us forget how cold we were but all that did was get him in trouble. There was a special news report on Channel 12 telling about how bad the weather was and Dad groaned when the guy said, "If you think it's cold now, wait until tonight, the temperature is expected to drop into record-low territory, possibly reaching the negative twenties! In fact, we won't be seeing anything above zero for the next four to five days!" He was smiling when he said this but none of the Watson family thought it was funny. We all looked over at Dad. He just shook his head and pulled the blanket over his eyes.

Then the guy on TV said, "Here's a little something we can use to brighten our spirits and give us some hope for the future: The temperature in Atlanta, Georgia, is forecast to reach . . ." Dad coughed real loud and jumped off the couch to turn the TV off but we all heard the weatherman say, ". . . the mid-seventies!" The guy might as well have tied Dad to a tree and said, "Ready, aim, fire!"

"Atlanta!" Momma said. "That's a hundred and fifty miles from home!"

"Wilona . . . ," Dad said.

"I knew it," Momma said. "I knew I should have listened to Moses Henderson!"

"Who?" I asked.

Dad said, "Oh Lord, not that sorry story. You've got to let me tell about what happened with him."

Momma said, "There's not a whole lot to tell, just a story about a young girl who made a bad choice. But if you do tell it, make sure you get all the facts right."

We all huddled as close as we could get because we knew Dad was going to try to make us forget about being cold by cutting up. Me and Joey started smiling right away, and Byron tried to look cool and bored.

"Kids," Dad said, "I almost wasn't your father. You guys came real close to having a clown for a daddy named Hambone Henderson. . . ."

"Daniel Watson, you stop right there. You're the one

who started that 'Hambone' nonsense. Before you started that everyone called him his Christian name, Moses. And he was a respectable boy too, he wasn't a clown at all."

"But the name stuck, didn't it? Hambone Henderson. Me and your granddaddy called him that because the boy had a head shaped just like a hambone, had more knots and bumps on his head than a dinosaur. So as you guys sit here giving me these dirty looks because it's a little chilly outside ask yourselves if you'd rather be a little cool or go through life being known as the Hambonettes."

Me and Joey cracked up, Byron kind of chuckled and Momma put her hand over her mouth. She did this whenever she was going to give a smile because she had a great big gap between her front teeth. If Momma thought something was funny, first you'd see her trying to keep her lips together to hide the gap, then, if the smile got to be too strong, you'd see the gap for a hot second before Momma's hand would come up to cover it, then she'd crack up too.

Laughing only encouraged Dad to cut up more, so when he saw the whole family thinking he was funny he really started putting on a show.

He stood in front of the TV. "Yup, Hambone Henderson proposed to your mother around the same time I did. Fought dirty too, told your momma a pack of lies about me and when she didn't believe them he told her a pack of lies about Flint."

Dad started talking Southern-style, imitating this

4

Hambone guy. "Wilona, I heard tell about the weather up that far north in Flint, Mitch-again, heard it's colder than inside a icebox. Seen a movie about it, think it was made in Flint. Movie called *Nanook of the North*. Yup, do believe for sure it was made in Flint. Uh-huh, Flint, Mitch-again.

"Folks there live in these things called igloos. According to what I seen in this here movie most the folks in Flint is Chinese. Don't believe I seen nan one colored person in the whole dang city. You a 'Bama gal, don't believe you'd be too happy living in no igloo. Ain't got nothing against 'em, but don't believe you'd be too happy living 'mongst a whole slew of Chinese folks. Don't believe you'd like the food. Only thing them Chinese folks in that movie et was whales and seals. Don't believe you'd like no whale meat. Don't taste a lick like chicken. Don't taste like pork at all."

Momma pulled her hand away from her mouth. "Daniel Watson, you are one lying man! Only thing you said that was true was that being in Flint is like living in a igloo. I knew I should have listened to Moses. Maybe these babies mighta been born with lumpy heads but at least they'da had *warm* lumpy heads!"

"You know Birmingham is a good place, and I don't mean just the weather either. The life is slower, the people are friendlier—"

"Oh yeah," Dad interrupted, "they're a laugh a minute down there. Let's see, where was that 'Coloreds Only' bathroom downtown?"

"Daniel, you know what I mean, things aren't perfect

but people are more honest about the way they feel"—
she took her mean eyes off Dad and put them on Byron—"and folks there do know how to respect their
parents."

Byron rolled his eyes like he didn't care. All he did
was tuck the blanket farther into the couch's cushion.

Dad didn't like the direction the conversation was
going so he called the landlord for the hundredth time.
The phone was still busy.

"That snake in the grass has got his phone off the
hook. Well, it's going to be too cold to stay here tonight, let me call Cydney. She just had that new furnace
put in, maybe we can spend the night there." Aunt
Cydney was kind of mean but her house was always
warm so we kept our fingers crossed that she was home.

Everyone, even Byron, cheered when Dad got Aunt
Cydney and she told us to hurry over before we froze to
death.

Dad went out to try and get the Brown Bomber
started. That was what we called our car. It was a 1948
Plymouth that was dull brown and real big, Byron said it
was turd brown. Uncle Bud gave it to Dad when it was
thirteen years old and we'd had it for two years. Me and
Dad took real good care of it but some of the time it
didn't like to start up in the winter.

After five minutes Dad came back in huffing and
puffing and slapping his arms across his chest.

"Well, it was touch and go for a while, but the Great
Brown One pulled through again!" Everyone cheered,

but me and Byron quit cheering and started frowning right away. By the way Dad smiled at us we knew what was coming next. Dad pulled two ice scrapers out of his pocket and said, "O.K., boys, let's get out there and knock those windows out."

We moaned and groaned and put some more coats on and went outside to scrape the car's windows. I could tell by the way he was pouting that Byron was going to try and get out of doing his share of the work.

"I'm not going to do your part, Byron, you'd better do it and I'm not playing either."

"Shut up, punk."

I went over to the Brown Bomber's passenger side and started hacking away at the scab of ice that was all over the windows. I finished Momma's window and took a break. Scraping ice off of windows when it's that cold can kill you!

I didn't hear any sound coming from the other side of the car so I yelled out, "I'm serious, Byron, I'm not doing that side too, and I'm only going to do half the windshield, I don't care what you do to me." The windshield on the Bomber wasn't like the new 1963 cars, it had a big bar running down the middle of it, dividing it in half.

"Shut your stupid mouth, I got something more important to do right now."

I peeked around the back of the car to see what By was up to. The only thing he'd scraped off was the outside mirror and he was bending down to look at himself in it. He saw me and said, "You know what, square? I must be adopted, there just ain't no way two folks as ugly as your momma and daddy coulda give birth to someone as sharp as me!"

He was running his hands over his head like he was brushing his hair.

I said, "Forget you," and went back over to the other side of the car to finish the back window. I had half of the ice off when I had to stop again and catch my breath. I heard Byron mumble my name.

I said, "You think I'm stupid? It's not going to work this time." He mumbled my name again. It sounded like his mouth was full of something. I knew this was a trick, I knew this was going to be How to Survive a Blizzard, Part Two.

How to Survive a Blizzard, Part One had been last night when I was outside playing in the snow and Byron and his running buddy, Buphead, came walking by. Buphead has officially been a juvenile delinquent even longer than Byron.

"Say, kid," By had said, "you wanna learn somethin' that might save your stupid life one day?"

I should have known better, but I was bored and I think maybe the cold weather was making my brain slow, so I said, "What's that?"

"We gonna teach you how to survive a blizzard."

"How?"

Byron put his hands in front of his face and said, "This is the most important thing to remember, O.K.?"

"Why?"

"Well, first we gotta show you what it feels like to be trapped in a blizzard. You ready?" He whispered something to Buphead and they both laughed.

"I'm ready."

I should have known that the only reason Buphead and By would want to play with me was to do something mean.

"O.K.," By said, "first thing you gotta worry about is high winds."

Byron and Buphead each grabbed one of my arms and one of my legs and swung me between them going, "*Wooo,* blizzard warnings! Blizzard warnings! *Wooo!* Take cover!"

Buphead counted to three and on the third swing they let me go in the air. I landed headfirst in a snowbank.

But that was O.K. because I had on three coats, two sweaters, a T-shirt, three pairs of pants and four socks along with a scarf, a hat and a hood. These guys couldn't have hurt me if they'd thrown me off the Empire State Building!

After I climbed out of the snowbank they started laughing and so did I.

"Cool, Baby Bruh," By said, "you passed that part of the test with a B-plus, what you think, Buphead?"

Buphead said, "Yeah, I'd give the little punk a A."

They whispered some more and started laughing again.

"O.K.," By said, "second thing you gotta learn is how to keep your balance in a high wind. You gotta be good at this so you don't get blowed into no polar bear dens."

They put me in between them and started making me spin round and round, it seemed like they spun me for about half an hour. When slob started flying out of my mouth they let me stop and I wobbled around for a while before they pushed me back in the same snowbank.

When everything stopped going in circles I got up and we all laughed again.

They whispered some more and then By said, "What you think, Buphead? He kept his balance a good long time, I'm gonna give him a A-minus."

"I ain't as hard a grader as you, I'ma give the little punk a double A-minus."

"O.K., Kenny, now the last part of Surviving a Blizzard, you ready?"

"Yup!"

"You passed the wind test and did real good on the balance test but now we gotta see if you ready to graduate. You remember what we told you was the most important part about survivin'?"

"Yup!"

"O.K., here we go. Buphead, tell him 'bout the final exam."

Buphead turned me around to look at him, putting my back to Byron. "O.K., square," he started, "I wanna make sure you ready for this one, you done so good so far I wanna make sure you don't blow it at graduation time. You think you ready?"

I nodded, getting ready to be thrown in the snow-bank real hard this time. I made up my mind I wasn't going to cry or anything, I made up my mind that no matter how hard they threw me in that snow I was going to get up laughing.

"O.K.," Buphead said, "everything's cool, you 'member what your brother said about puttin' your hands up?"

"Like this?" I covered my face with my gloves.

"Yeah, that's it!" Buphead looked over my shoulder at Byron and then said, "*Wooo!* High winds, blowing snow! *Wooo!* Look out! Blizzard a-comin'! Death around the corner! Look out!"

Byron mumbled my name and I turned around to see why his voice sounded so funny. As soon as I looked at him Byron blasted me in the face with a mouthful of snow.

Man! It was hard to believe how much stuff By could put in his mouth! Him and Buphead just about died laughing as I stood there with snow and spit and ice dripping off of my face.

Byron caught his breath and said, "Aww, man, you flunked! You done so good, then you go and flunk the Blowin' Snow section of How to Survive a Blizzard, you forgot to put your hands up! What you say, Buphead, F?"

"Yeah, double F-minus!"

It was a good thing my face was numb from the cold

already or I might have froze to death. I was too embarrassed about getting tricked to tell on them so I went in the house and watched TV.

So as me and By scraped the ice off the Brown Bomber I wasn't going to get fooled again. I kept on chopping ice off the back window and ignored By's mumbling voice.

The next time I took a little rest Byron was still calling my name but sounding like he had something in his mouth. He was saying, "Keh-ee! Keh-ee! Hel' . . . hel' . . . !" When he started banging on the door of the car I went to take a peek at what was going on.

By was leaned over the outside mirror, looking at something in it real close. Big puffs of steam were coming out of the side of the mirror.

I picked up a big, hard chunk of ice to get ready for Byron's trick.

"Keh-ee! Keh-ee! Hel' me! Hel' me! Go geh Momma! Go geh Mom-ma! Huwwy uh!"

"I'm not playing, Byron! I'm not that stupid! You'd better start doing your side of the car or I'll tear you up with this iceball."

He banged his hand against the car harder and started stomping his feet. "Oh, please, Keh-ee! Hel' me, go geh Mom-ma!"

I raised the ice chunk over my head. "I'm not playing, By, you better get busy or I'm telling Dad."

I moved closer and when I got right next to him I could see boogers running out of his nose and tears running down his cheeks. These weren't tears from the cold either, these were big juicy crybaby tears! I dropped my ice chunk.

"By! What's wrong?"

"Hel' me! Keh-ee! Go geh hel'!"

I moved closer. I couldn't believe my eyes! Byron's mouth was frozen on the mirror! He was as stuck as a fly on flypaper!

I could have done a lot of stuff to him. If it had been me with my lips stuck on something like this he'd have tortured me for a couple of days before he got help. Not me, though, I nearly broke my neck trying to get into the house to rescue Byron.

As soon as I ran through the front door Momma, Dad and Joey all yelled, "Close that door!"

"Momma, quick! It's By! He's froze up outside!"

No one seemed too impressed.

I screamed, "Really! He's froze to the car! Help! He's crying!"

That shook them up. You could cut Byron's head off and he probably wouldn't cry.

"Kenneth Bernard Watson, what on earth are you talking about?"

"Momma, please hurry up!"

Momma, Dad and Joey threw on some extra coats and followed me to the Brown Bomber.

The fly was still stuck and buzzing. "Oh, Mom-ma! Hel' me! Geh me offa 'ere!"

"Oh my Lord!" Momma screamed, and I thought

she was going to do one of those movie-style faints, she even put her hand over her forehead and staggered back a little bit.

Joey, of course, started crying right along with Byron.

Dad was doing his best not to explode laughing. Big puffs of smoke were coming out of his nose and mouth as he tried to squeeze his laughs down. Finally he put his head on his arms and leaned against the car's hood and howled.

"Byron," Momma said, gently wiping tears off his cheeks with the end of her scarf, "it's O.K., sweetheart, how'd this happen?" She sounded like she was going to be crying in a minute herself.

Dad raised his head and said, "Why are you asking how it happened? Can't you tell, Wilona? This little knucklehead was kissing his reflection in the mirror and got his lips stuck!" Dad took a real deep breath. "Is your tongue stuck too?"

"No! Quit teasin', Da-ee! Hel'! Hel'!"

"Well, at least the boy hadn't gotten too passionate with himself!" Dad thought that was hilarious and put his head back on his arms.

Momma didn't see anything funny. "Daniel Watson! What are we gonna do?